"Breakfast is almost ready,"

Kate called.

Dylan came in, fastening his shirt. "You don't have to cook for me. I don't expect it."

"I don't mind."

"At least you should wear something a little less...that is, something more suitable for cooking."

Perplexed, Kate looked down at her nightshirt. "What's wrong with this?"

"For one thing, there's nothing to protect your skin," Dylan growled. "Your legs are completely bare."

"Not really. See?" She plucked at the nightshirt, pulling it higher. The shirt went halfway down her thighs.

"For God's sake, don't do that!"

Dear Reader,

Whether our heroes are flirting with their best friends or taking care of adorable tots, their stories of falling for the right woman are sure to melt your heart. Don't miss one magical moment of this month's collection from Silhouette Romance.

Carolyn Zane begins THE BRUBAKER BRIDES miniseries by introducing us to the first of three Texas-bred sisters, in *Virginia's Getting Hitched* (SR #1730). Dr. Virginia Brubaker knows the secret to a long-lasting relationship: compatibility. But one sexy, irreverent ranch hand has a different theory all together…that he hopes to test on the prim but not-so-proper doctor!

In *Just Between Friends* (SR #1731), the latest emotion-packed tale from Julianna Morris, a handsome contractor rescues his well-to-do best friend by agreeing to marry her—for a year. But he doesn't know about her little white lie—for them, she's always wanted more than friendship.…

Prince Perfect always answers the call of duty…to his sons and to his kingdom. But his beautiful nanny tempts him to let go of his inhibitions and give in to the call of the heart. Find out if this bachelor dad will make the perfect husband, in *Falling for Prince Federico* (SR #1732) by Nicole Burnham.

The newest title from Holly Jacobs, *Be My Baby* (SR #1733), promises a rollicking good time! When a carefree single guy finds a baby on his doorstep, he's sure things couldn't get worse—until he's stranded in a snowstorm with his annoyingly attractive receptionist. With sparks flying, they're guaranteed to stay warm!

Sincerely,

Mavis C. Allen
Associate Senior Editor

Please address questions and book requests to:
Silhouette Reader Service
U.S.: 3010 Walden Ave., P.O. Box 1325, Buffalo, NY 14269
Canadian: P.O. Box 609, Fort Erie, Ont. L2A 5X3

Just Between Friends

JULIANNA MORRIS

SILHOUETTE *Romance*®

Published by Silhouette Books

America's Publisher of Contemporary Romance

To my sister.
Thanks for pitching in…even when it wasn't fun.

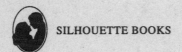 SILHOUETTE BOOKS

ISBN 0-373-19731-4

JUST BETWEEN FRIENDS

Copyright © 2004 by Julianna Morris

This edition published by arrangement with Harlequin Books S.A.

® and TM are trademarks of Harlequin Books S.A., used under license.
Trademarks indicated with ® are registered in the United States Patent
and Trademark Office, the Canadian Trade Marks Office and in other
countries.

Visit Silhouette Books at www.eHarlequin.com

Printed in U.S.A.

Books by Julianna Morris

Silhouette Romance

Baby Talk #1097
Family of Three #1178
Daddy Woke Up Married #1252
Dr. Dad #1278
The Marriage Stampede #1375
*Callie, Get Your Groom #1436
*Hannah Gets a Husband #1448
*Jodie's Mail-Order Man #1460
Meeting Megan Again #1502
Tick Tock Goes the Baby Clock #1531
Last Chance for Baby! #1565
A Date with a Billionaire #1590
The Right Twin for Him #1676
The Bachelor Boss #1703
Just Between Friends #1731

*Bridal Fever!

JULIANNA MORRIS

has an offbeat sense of humor, which frequently gets her into trouble. She is often accused of being curious about everything. Her interests range from oceanography and photography to traveling, antiquing, walking on the beach and reading science fiction.

Julianna loves cats of all shapes and sizes, and recently she was adopted by a feline companion named Merlin. Like his namesake, Merlin is an alchemist—she says he can transform the house into a disaster area in nothing flat. And since he shares the premises with a writer, it's interesting to note that he's particularly fond of knocking books on the floor.

Julianna happily reports meeting her Mr. Right. Together they are working on a new dream of building a shoreline home in the Great Lakes area.

THE O'ROURKE FAMILY TREE

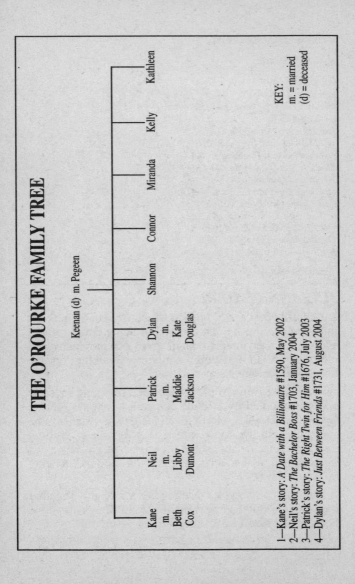

Keenan (d) m. Pegeen

Kane
m.
Beth
Cox

Neil
m.
Libby
Dumont

Patrick
m.
Maddie
Jackson

Dylan
m.
Kate
Douglas

Shannon

Connor

Miranda

Kelly

Kathleen

KEY:
m. = married
(d) = deceased

1—Kane's story: *A Date with a Billionaire* #1590, May 2002
2—Neil's story: *The Bachelor Boss* #1703, January 2004
3—Patrick's story: *The Right Twin for Him* #1676, July 2003
4—Dylan's story: *Just Between Friends* #1731, August 2004

Chapter One

"**I**'m sorry, you can't go in."

Dylan O'Rourke heard his secretary's protest a split second before the door opened. He spun his chair around, prepared to deal with an insistent client, and saw Kate Douglas instead.

"Kate."

She smiled. "Hey, Dylan."

"What do you want?"

With Kate it was wise to cut to the chase. When they were kids he'd had an annoying habit of being unable to say "no" to the lady—like the time she'd gotten him to help her run away from home. He still remembered his father's blistering lecture over that particular stunt. After that Dylan had nicknamed her "Katydid," to remind himself that he didn't have to do everything that Kate did.

"Right now I want to sit down."

Kate sank onto the couch and crossed her legs. Her long gold hair matched the earrings and the gold chain around her neck, and she wore a white silk dress, white silk hose and a pair of white leather sandals…an outfit that probably cost more than his first car.

White, in a construction office.

Dylan shook his head, yet he couldn't help grinning at the same time. Common dirt wouldn't dare stick to someone with Katrina Douglas's kind of old money— gold dust, maybe, but never just plain dirt.

"It's good to see you," Kate said softly.

"Same here." And he meant it. Kate might be a spoiled rich kid, but she was bright and full of fun…and she could wheedle a glass of water from a man lost in the desert.

Of course, he was older now, and not nearly so susceptible. He usually got stuck with buying tickets to some god-awful charity event when she stopped by to see him, but he'd refused other stuff. Like the time she'd wanted to auction him as a bachelor at one of her fund-raisers. Dylan shuddered at the memory. He was willing to escort her now and then to a party, but get auctioned?

Not a chance.

"What is it, Kate?" he asked, determined to get right to the heart of the matter. "Another fund-raiser? I'll donate, but I'm not coming."

"No, it isn't another fund-raiser. Though it was mean of you not to show up at the last one. You were supposed to be my date."

"No, I wasn't. I told you I couldn't go to that one, you just didn't listen."

She didn't look convinced. "There I was, all alone," she said. "It was terrible—it's humiliating to be the only woman without an escort."

Dylan almost fell into the trap before he caught the sparkle in her green eyes. "Brat," he muttered.

"So, why couldn't you come?"

"I was busy. And I'm tired of dry sandwiches with the crusts cut off."

"They weren't dry."

"They're always dry. You've dragged me to enough of those things for me to know I'll be poorly fed and miserably uncomfortable. Honest, Katydid, you have the most boring friends. And they have an insatiable curiosity about how you happen to know an immigrant Irish construction worker. I should wear a sign that says My Dad Was One of the Help. Maybe I'd get left in peace."

"Strictly speaking, your *parents* were the immigrants. You were born in the United States."

"You know what I mean."

"And you own the construction company," Kate added. "You're a very successful businessman."

"Don't glamorize me. I'm still a construction worker, and your friends wouldn't know the difference between the working end of a hammer and a staple gun."

"Maybe they're curious because you're Kane O'Rourke's brother," she said brightly.

Dylan snorted. His brother had become one of the wealthiest men in the country, but to the Douglases' small and snobbish social circle, it was new money and not worth their attention. Of course, some of the unattached women he'd met at those fund-raisers had obviously hoped for an introduction to Kane, at least before he'd gotten married.

Thank God Kane had found a genuinely sweet and loving woman. Beth was terrific—down-to-earth and totally unimpressed with her husband's money.

"Or maybe everyone wonders what such a great-looking guy is doing with *me*," Kate suggested.

She did her best to look pathetic, but Dylan wasn't buying a second of it. If he hadn't watched her grow up from a skinny little kid, Kate's golden-haired beauty would probably knock him breathless. Instead he was merely wary.

"Then when you *don't* escort me," she continued sadly, "I'll bet they think you found someone prettier."

"Give me a break," Dylan muttered.

He didn't usually think about the way Kate had blossomed. He wasn't even sure when it had happened. One minute she was a bratty kid with a genius for talking him into trouble, the next minute she was dropping male jaws all over Seattle. But she still seemed awfully young—mostly because of the impish mischief lurking in her sea green eyes.

After a moment Kate looked up, but for once her eyes were very serious. "What you said about the 'help'…does it bother you that your father used to work for my family?"

"Not particularly. Your friends, on the other hand?" Dylan lifted a shoulder.

"We might work on fund-raising projects together, but they're my mother's friends," Kate said slowly. "I don't fit in that well."

"You're young, give it a couple years."

Frustrated, Kate regarded the tips of her toes, then wiggled them inside her sandals. Dylan was only two years older, yet he treated her like a little kid. Nothing she did seemed to make a difference to the way he saw her. She'd long since given up hoping that he'd look into her eyes and discover she was the woman of his dreams, but the least he could do was realize she'd grown up.

Honestly, it was so irritating.

She was a leftover piece of his childhood, someone he considered too immature, too flighty and too rich and spoiled to be anything but a friend. Men could be so blind when it came to women.

"I won't fit in with mother's friends if I live to be a hundred," she declared, prompting a chuckle from Dylan.

"God, Katydid, you do make me laugh," he said, settling back in his chair.

Kate sighed. Dylan didn't laugh enough, not since his father's death. He was so serious about everything, he needed someone to shake up his life…and she was *just* the one to do the shaking. And if he'd only realized it before now, she wouldn't have to go to such ridiculous lengths to get his attention.

The O'Rourkes had been part of her world since before she could remember. She'd adored them from the beginning, and Dylan in particular. Keenan O'Rourke had worked seven days a week—five days for a forestry company, and two days as a handyman for her parents, but he'd always seemed to have time for his kids. Quite a contrast to *her* father, who'd been born wealthy, didn't work, and rarely noticed her at all.

Dylan began looking through some papers on his desk, giving every indication that he'd forgotten she was in the room. Kate's stomach clenched. Was she totally nuts, wanting him to decide she was Miss Right and fall desperately in love with her? Or would she just be getting one more inattentive man in her life even if he *did* decide he was in love?

"*Dylan,*" Kate said insistently.

He looked up. "Goodness, where did you come from, Katydid?" He grinned, then winked.

"You…rat," she growled, but she wasn't really angry. So Dylan had been playing a joke on her, she should have known he wouldn't forget she was around. If nothing else, he'd been taught too much courtesy by his parents.

He put the papers back on his desk and crossed his arms over his flat stomach. "All right, kiddo, no more fooling around. What do you want? We've already ruled out one of your fund-raisers, but that leaves plenty of territory."

Kate bit the inside of her lip and tried to look innocent. "Do I need a reason to visit my best friend?"

"Hah," he scoffed. "I'm only your best friend when you want something. So stop stalling and let me have it."

"So you can say no, right?"

"Yes." Dylan scowled. "That is, no, I don't always refuse. In fact, I say yes way too often when it comes to you. You're a spoiled brat. Do you know that?"

"Whatever you say." Kate wrinkled her nose. She might be spoiled by having too much money, but she'd trade every penny to be part of Dylan's family. They were real and loving and took care of each other, no matter what. And Dylan *was* her best friend, even if he didn't realize it.

"Katydid?"

Taking a deep breath, she tossed her head back.

"The name is Kate or Katrina. I stopped being Katydid a long time ago." Actually, Dylan was the only one who'd ever called her Katydid, and she didn't really mind except that it meant he still saw her as a child.

"You're stalling."

Of course she was stalling. He wasn't going to like what she had in mind, but if she was careful about how she suggested it, he might agree. "You remember that my grandmother died several months ago?" she asked.

Dylan nodded. In his opinion Jane Elmira Douglas had been the Wicked Witch of the West's less likable sister, but Katydid was softhearted enough to have loved the old bat, regardless. He'd gone over to see Kate the night of the funeral and even though she'd smiled and pretended it was all right, her eyes had been sad and bruised looking.

"Yes, it's been about six months," he said.

"That's right."

"And...?" Dylan prodded, as gently as possible.

"Uh, well, it's my birthday next month."

"I know." A small frown gathered on his forehead. He was surprised she'd brought it up; ever since Kate's parents had forgotten her sweet-sixteenth, she'd been a little touchy about the day.

She stirred restlessly, tugging at her white dress and smoothing the skirt. He waited, knowing that sooner or later she'd tell him what was going on—there was always a plan behind Kate's verbal detours. As a kid he'd spent a lot of time bemused by the way she flitted around, the bright, elegant butterfly to his ordinary caterpillar. Now he mostly crossed his arms and sat back until she lighted on something.

"My birthday was mentioned in Grandmamma's will. And that's sort of the problem."

"I see," he said, though he didn't see at all.

"She left me the Douglas Hill House, but only if I get married by my twenty-seventh birthday. I'm twenty-six now, so I don't have much time."

Dylan blinked. The Douglas Hill House was a mansion that overlooked the city of Seattle like a brooding raven and had to be the ugliest place ever built. He'd been inside it once when Kate had dragged him to an interminable party to raise money for disabled children. The only bright spot had been watching her play with the kids. She was great with youngsters; someday she ought to have a big family of her own.

"You're going to be twenty-seven?" he asked.

Kate rolled her eyes. Dylan was an intelligent man, surely he had an inkling of what she wanted.

"Yes, I'm going to be twenty-seven. And Grandmamma was worried that I'd never marry, so that's why she put the provision in the will. I get the final deed after a year of marriage." Kate crossed her fingers because the next part was sort of a lie. "She knew I'd do anything to keep the house in the family."

"Yeah, of course. You love the old place."

She loved it, all right.

She'd love to see it dynamited.

Her grandmother had never had a clue about what her granddaughter wanted. The hardest part about losing Nanna Jane was knowing she'd been a disappointing afterthought to her own grandmother—never quite refined or proper enough to fulfill the Douglas legacy.

You're just like your great-grandfather. You have no

respect for our position, Nanna Jane would say, her lips pursed with disapproval.

Kate couldn't remember the first time she'd heard the accusation, and it had taken years of digging and putting facts together before she learned what her grandmother meant. After his wife had died and his children were grown, Rycroft Douglas had gone to Alaska to dig for gold. The fact that her great-grandfather had added considerably to the family fortune hadn't mitigated the outrageous scandal of a *Douglas* becoming a flamboyant adventurer.

Jiminy, Kate envied him.

She'd found Rycroft's letters to his son, written from the Alaskan gold fields. The old man had been having the time of his life—much to the disapproval of his straitlaced daughter-in-law, who couldn't quite embrace the idea that Seattle was basically a frontier town turned shipping capital. Kate didn't know. Maybe certain owners of Seattle's old money needed to be more uptight than their counterparts in places like Boston because their money wasn't quite as old as they'd like it to be. Or maybe old money was the same everywhere.

Well, at least Nanna Jane's will was giving her a chance to get what *she* wanted—though it was hardly what her grandmother must have planned.

"You understand my problem?" Kate said, a questioning note to her voice.

Dylan nodded. "More or less. You have a little over a month to get married."

"But I don't have anyone I *want* to marry."

All at once suspicion grew in his face. "Now, Kate, you aren't thinking...dammit, you *aren't* thinking what I think you're thinking."

"But it's the perfect solution."

"For you, maybe. It's a disaster for me."

She didn't have to manufacture tears, the implied insult was more than enough to make her cry. "That's a terrible thing to say. A lot of men want to marry me."

"Then marry one of them!"

"But they'd want a real marriage. I just need a husband for a year." A tear dripped down her cheek.

"Now, Katydid, don't start."

A second tear joined the first. "We're friends, and friends help each other."

"Not that way. It's out of the question."

Out of the question in that tone of voice didn't sound good, and she swallowed. She'd hoped so much that this would work. But she wasn't going to give up, not yet.

"I'd just hate to lose Grandmamma's house. There's so much family history there, and all that…uh…hardwood and parquet flooring." Kate nearly gagged. If the house was completely renovated it might be a lovely home, but presently it was grim and depressing, a reflection of the austere woman who'd lived there for sixty-seven years.

"So bite the bullet and marry someone else."

"But that would be the same as selling myself, just to get the house." She tried to appear shocked. "How can you possibly suggest such a thing?" She actually *was* shocked, though women had been marrying men for money and position and property for much longer than she'd been around.

Dylan clenched his fingers. Truthfully, he wasn't wild about the notion of Kate marrying one of the stuffed shirts who were always buzzing around her. He supposed it was because he was like a big brother to Katydid, and brothers never approved of their sister's boyfriends. But there wasn't any way he was going along with her nutty scheme.

Kate pulled a white handkerchief from her white purse and dabbed her eyes. "You want me to act like a prostitute, trading my body for gain. It wouldn't be any different."

"That's not what I meant," Dylan said, appalled.

"Yes, it is." She lifted her chin. "Fine, if that's what you want, I'll decide which one of them I'm going to marry. You'll get an invitation to the wedding."

With a graceful twist of her body she rose from the couch and headed for the door.

She looked over her shoulder. "Maybe you can be best man," she said as a parting shot. "I'm sure it's an honor you deserve."

The door closed behind her and Dylan groaned and thumped his head against his high-backed chair. She was working on his guilt and trying to make him feel responsible for a situation he had no part in creating.

Still, in a way Katydid was right. It *would* be selling herself to get the house. She plainly wasn't in love with any of those suitors she'd talked about, and they would expect far more from the marriage than she wanted to give.

Suddenly he couldn't bear the thought of sweet little Katydid submitting to a man's attentions simply because her grandmother had been a conniving witch. There had to be another way. The Douglases' small social circle wasn't populated with a single man worth a red cent in terms of character. And several of those guys

weren't very nice beneath their silk shirts and mono-
grammed money clips.

Dylan rushed to his feet and hurried through the outer
office. He caught up with Kate on the street below just
as she was getting into her disreputable car. Why she insisted on driving the beat-up old Volkswagen Beetle
was beyond him. Granted, it was a classic, but the least
she could do was have the thing properly restored. He
supposed it was her way of rebelling.

"Kate, wait."

She turned and the look on her face made him wince.

"What? More advice?" Her chin rose higher. "Believe me, I have all the advice I need from you."

"Please, Katydid, we need to talk."

"I think we've said everything. Of course, I won't be
bothering you anymore to buy fund-raising tickets. I
don't suppose that my husband, whoever he turns out
to be, would like it anymore than he'd like you showing up to watch something on the VCR with us."

Damn.

Dylan's fingers itched with the illogical urge to throt-
tle Kate's theoretical husband. It would be a pain tying
himself to a spoiled princess for a year, but on the other
hand, he'd watched after Kate since they were children.
Like the time he'd talked her down from the roof of her
parents' six-car garage after she'd convinced herself
that she was really a fairy with invisible wings.

"Kate, there isn't *one* man you've dated who you feel
some affection for?"

Something flickered deep in her eyes—an emotion
he'd never seen before—but it disappeared and he decided he must have been mistaken.

"There's no one else."

He let out a breath. "Maybe you could suggest the same arrangement to one of those guys, and they'd agree."

"But you're the only one I trust," she said simply.

Oh, God.

He supposed it really *was* that simple. "Look, I'll come over tonight, and we'll talk about it some more. *Talk*, that's all. I'm not making any promises."

Kate hesitated, wanting to push, but she knew it would just make Dylan more unwilling, which was the last thing she wanted now that he seemed to be considering her proposal. "All right. I'll order Chinese."

"Nope, the last time you got calamari. Damn stuff was so rubbery my jaw ached for a week. I'll bring pizza."

She nodded and put her key in the lock. Asking a man to marry her was much harder than getting him to help her run away from home or go to another boring fundraiser. She'd like to believe that Dylan—who said he was allergic to marriage—was really crazy about her and didn't know it. But Kate had learned not to fool herself. She just prayed that living together for a year would convince him that she was the love of his life.

If necessary, she'd resort to drastic measures. How hard could it be to seduce a man who's bumping up against you day and night? But then, maybe she didn't want to know. Dylan had always been depressingly resistant to her in that way.

"I'll see you later," she said.

"Yeah, maybe we can discuss why you won't get a proper car for yourself."

Kate patted the steering wheel of the VW. She loved her car. It had character. She'd bought it with the advance from the sale of her first children's book. Hardly anybody knew she worked; it was one of the few things that was hers alone. Dylan might find out if they got married, but then again, maybe not.

It wasn't like they'd be sharing a bedroom or anything. Darn it.

Chapter Two

"It's the pizza guy."

Kate's pulse jumped at the sound of Dylan's voice coming from the other side of the front door. She took a last look at herself in the mirror and smoothed a strand of hair at her temple.

She'd taken great pains to dress casually in off-the-rack clothing. There wasn't any need to remind him about her family's money. Of course, he was very successful now, and his oldest brother's current financial status made the Douglas fortune look like pocket change, but that didn't alter the fact that at one time she'd been rich when he was poor.

"I hope that pizza is still hot," she said, opening the door. "I don't tip for cold deliveries."

Dylan grinned. "You shouldn't open the door without being sure it isn't some weirdo on the other side."

"I knew it was you, so there wasn't any doubt it was a weirdo."

"You have a real way about you, Katydid."

Kate stepped back so he could enter. Dylan always seemed so big to her, maybe because he topped her by at least ten inches and eighty pounds of muscle. Lord, he gave her a weak feeling in the tummy. He wasn't as perfectly handsome as his brothers, but he had a raw sexuality that was powerful and completely irresistible.

A secret smile tugged at her mouth.

Dylan's rugged good looks caused a stir wherever he went. It wasn't any wonder that the women he met at fund-raisers were curious about him, and more than a little envious when she showed up on his arm. Of course, the old guard of her grandmother's generation could be snotty, but she'd seen them bowled over by his charm, nevertheless.

"I brought some wine," Dylan said, waving a bag.

"Okay," Kate said unenthusiastically.

He chuckled. "Don't worry, I know you prefer milk with pizza." Instead of a wine bottle, he pulled a carton of milk from the bag.

Just like that, he made her feel ten years old again. Milk was for little girls and kittens, not sophisticated women.

"Maybe I'll have beer tonight," she muttered, walking into her kitchen. The converted apartment over the garage was the one place on her grandmother's estate that she liked. The garage had once been a carriage house with living quarters above, and it was hidden from the main house by a stand of trees. She had a private entrance to the estate, so her friends had been able to visit without being scrutinized by Nanna Jane.

Really, her grandmother should have worked for the CIA. She would have made a great spy.

Dylan set the pizza box on the old farm-kitchen table she'd rescued from a junk heap. Kate automatically opened the cupboard to get some plates, then shook her head. Dylan always said regular people didn't eat pizza off plates—they just grabbed a napkin and chowed down.

"Have you...mmm...decided..." Her voice trailed, instincts telling her that he wasn't ready to discuss anything beyond dinner. "That is, do you want beer or wine? I have your favorite beer, and I think I have some red wine, too."

Dylan restrained his grin. "Milk is fine. You don't need to have a drink on my account."

"I'm over twenty-one, I can drink alcohol."

"Yeah, but you don't like it."

She gave him a narrow look that announced he was on extremely thin ice. "This is about you thinking I'm still a child, right?"

"Chugging beer isn't going to change my opinion one way or the other," Dylan murmured. Kate was so cute with her feathers ruffled that he enjoyed shaking her up now and then.

She thumped two glasses on the table. "You're impossible. A total pill."

"I know."

Dylan spied a smile tugging at the corners of her mouth and shook his head. She really was a sweet kid.

All afternoon he'd been thinking about her crazy plan to get married. He supposed that it was natural Kate would turn to him for help—he'd been playing protective big brother ever since they'd met. Despite her family's money, she'd had a lonely childhood, spending more time with the family servants than with her family. When he'd come with his dad to wash the cars and do yard work she'd tagged along, always at his heels, asking questions and making him feel…

He sighed.

Might as well admit it, Kate had made him feel big and important, even though he was just a skinny youngster wearing hand-me-down jeans and T-shirts. In a funny sort of way she still made him feel big and important whenever they were together, teasing and calling him her best friend.

"Such a serious face." Kate opened the carton of milk and filled their glasses. "If you behave yourself you can have a wine milkshake later."

"And if I don't behave, what do I get then?" Dylan's voice deepened provocatively, startling him.

Where had *that* come from?

He'd never flirted with Kate. She was a bright, annoying kid who he was fond of, but he'd never considered anything romantic with her. Heck, he'd seen her knobby knees when she was a youngster and listened as she bemoaned her flat chest. Not that she was flat-chested any longer. In fact, she had a very nice set of measurements. So nice it was…he hastily put a brake on his unruly thoughts.

Kate blinked, obviously surprised. Then she tossed her head and gave him a slow smile. "You'll get something better than a wine milkshake, that's for sure."

Dylan didn't have time to decipher the expression in her eyes before she spun around and grabbed a shaker of crushed red pepper from the counter.

"Do you want fresh-grated Parmesan on your pizza?" she asked over her shoulder.

"Uh…I think they included some. Not fresh-grated, but good enough," he muttered, still trying to sort out what had just happened. For God's sake, he'd actually been flirting with a girl he regarded as a kid sister. Romance with Kate had never occurred to him, and if it had, he would have laughed at the idea. She was too rich, too flighty, too everything.

"Okay."

She set the hot pepper sprinkles next to his glass of milk, which made him grin despite his inner turmoil. Kate didn't like spicy food, which was why he always ordered their pizza as half vegetarian and half meat-lover's special. She'd eat a couple pieces of the vegetarian and he'd have the rest.

Yet his smile faded as he gazed at the table. Kate had bought a special shaker and filled it with crushed red pepper after the time the restaurant had forgotten to include any with their order. She might be a royal pain, but she was fiercely loyal to her friends. Nothing was too much trouble when Kate Douglas was on your side.

A stab of guilt hit Dylan. Was it really such a sacrifice to marry her for a year? They got along pretty well, and it wasn't as if he was dating anyone seriously. In fact, a convenient not-really-a-marriage with Kate would get his mother off his back about finding a nice girl. Now that three of her children were happily wed, Pegeen O'Rourke was even more determined to see the rest of them married off. It was something to think about.

"Earth to Dylan," Kate intoned, jolting him back to

the present. She dropped into a chair and rested her chin on her hand. "I'm hungry, how about you?"

"Right," he muttered. "Hungry."

A spicy fragrance rose from the large pizza inside the box, and they ate quietly for several minutes. Silences between them had always been comfortable and natural, but Kate's earlier proposal had changed all that. He was crazy to even consider marrying a spoiled princess with the staying power of a soap bubble. Everything about her was delicate, from her golden hair and sea-green eyes to the arches in her small feet. She didn't have a clue about the tough things in life.

Of course, if they *did* get married it wouldn't be real. They'd be like roommates, with separate lives and separate beds. Legally, they'd end with a divorce, but as far as his conscience was concerned, it would be an annulment. A marriage that hasn't been consummated isn't a marriage in the first place.

"You aren't having any hot pepper," Kate said, shifting uncomfortably.

She couldn't understand the peculiar expression on Dylan's face or the way he stared at her. It wasn't desire or affection—more like she had spinach caught in her teeth.

He shook the red pepper on his pizza and continued eating. She glanced around her cozy home and thought about what it would be like to share it with someone. She'd hate losing the carriage house because of Nanna Jane's will, but it would be worse to lose her best friend. Maybe she should just tell Dylan she'd changed her mind and was giving up the estate.

Yet when Kate opened her mouth, the words stuck

in her throat. She didn't want to spend the rest of her life wondering about what might have been. It was hard enough having spent her entire adult life pining after a man who thought she was still a kid. So instead of saying anything, she bit into a second slice of pizza.

She wanted to be like Great-Grandfather Rycroft Douglas, who threw his hat in the wind and dug for gold in the land of the midnight sun. That's where she wanted to spend her honeymoon, in Alaska, celebrating the rebellious spirit she'd inherited from him.

All at once the corners of Kate's mouth turned down. *If* she married Dylan—and it was a big if—there wouldn't be a real honeymoon. Darn it all. She didn't know whether to be angry about the conditions in Nanna Jane's will or grateful for the opportunity.

"What's wrong, Katydid?" Dylan asked quietly. "Are you thinking about your grandmother's will?"

Her startled gaze flew to his. "How did you…?"

"I can tell you're unhappy about something, and that's the most obvious cause."

Well, she *had* been thinking about the will in connection to Dylan and what the future might bring. Her spirits lifted. He'd sensed she was unhappy. It wasn't a declaration of love, but it was better than nothing.

Kate shrugged and drank the last of her milk. "I'm all right," she said noncommittally. She knew enough about Dylan to know she couldn't push.

He reached across the table and drew his thumb across her upper lip. Heat rose in her cheeks both from his touch and the realization that she'd left a thin line of milk on her mouth. Lord, what her grandmother would have said about such unladylike impropriety.

Kate didn't care about the impropriety, but she hated looking ridiculous. Yet Dylan's dark eyes were curiously warm.

"Dylan?" she whispered.

For a long moment he just stared at her lips. The breath caught in her throat and a tingling sensation crept across her nerves. Was he thinking about kissing her, or just wondering what it would be like? She'd only thought about it a few thousand times, but who was counting?

"I…I've been thinking about what you said…suggested this afternoon," he muttered. "If we do it, we'll need to sign a prenuptial agreement. It should be clear when we end things that we each keep what we owned before the marriage. Your grandmother's lawyers can draft the thing—they'll probably insist on it, anyway."

The hope cascading through Kate came to a crashing halt.

A prenuptial agreement?

That's what he'd been thinking about?

"You think I'd try to take part of your business?" she gasped. "How could you even begin to think such a thing? I don't want a penny of your money. That's absolutely the most ridiculous, unbeliev—"

"Whoa." Dylan clamped his hand over her mouth. "Dammit, that isn't what I meant. Your grandmother's property alone must be worth more than my construction business, not to mention your trust fund and everything else. I'd just want to make it clear that I'm not interested in your family fortune."

Annoyed, Kate nipped the callused palm of his hand with her teeth. He yanked his hand away with a low growl.

"So you want to save your pride with a pre-nup," she snapped. "Announce to the whole wide world that you don't think our marriage will last. Shall we publish the details in the *Seattle Times* classifieds, or do you think a simple announcement to our friends and families will be enough?"

Frustrated, Dylan ran his fingers through his hair. "It wouldn't be a real marriage, so what does it matter what everyone thinks?"

She gave him a baleful look.

If Dylan didn't already know what mattered, he probably wouldn't ever know. It wasn't just wounded pride—though her pride was already plenty wounded—it was something more fundamental. Dylan was her best friend; she trusted him in ways she'd never trusted anyone. She didn't want a prenuptial agreement because legal agreements were for people who didn't trust each other.

Unfortunately, she needed a reason that a pragmatist like Dylan O'Rourke would accept.

"It has to *look* like a real marriage," she said. "Or the lawyers will make trouble. A pre-nup might seem suspicious."

Dylan frowned. "Won't they want to protect you just in case? At the very least your father will insist on me signing something. I don't think he likes me that much."

A pang went through Kate. Her father wasn't the protective type—sometimes she wondered if he remembered her name.

"I doubt it," she said dryly. "Father and Mother are in Europe for a few months. I doubt they'll even come back for the wedding."

"Katy—"

"It doesn't matter," Kate said hastily, not wanting Dylan to feel sorry for her. "But you should know that Grandmamma's will says we have to live on the property for a year as husband and wife." It was the truth, and she was quite certain her grandmother's snooty lawyers would scrutinize the situation like a gaggle of gossiping old biddies.

"You mean we have to live in that mausoleum?" Dylan groaned.

Kate's heart jumped because it sounded as if he'd decided to help her. "The will just says we have to live on the property, so I thought we'd stay here in my place."

"Here?"

"It seems easiest, especially since the big house needs a huge amount of work to be comfortable," she said, trying to sound practical. Dylan was the kind of man who'd want a practical wife, and she had every intention of being the best wife in the world. "We'll just be housemates. Of course, everyone has to believe it's a real marriage," she added hastily.

He glanced around her kitchen with an unreadable expression. "Your place is a little small," he murmured.

Well, *duh.*

The last thing Kate wanted was to move into Nanna Jane's mansion with its dozens of cold rooms and echoing space. She wanted them to live in a place where Dylan couldn't avoid her, no matter how hard he tried.

It wasn't as if she was being terribly deceitful, or anything. If he really thought about it, he'd realize how she'd been in love with him forever. And if he still didn't feel the same about her after being married for a year, she'd agree to an uncontested divorce.

But Dylan was still looking thoughtful, so she pushed aside the possibility of failure and leaned forward. "What's wrong with my place? It's not that small and your company did the work to modernize it, so you know it's in good condition."

"Hmm…yes." He scratched the side of his face. "But this is a great old building and there's a lot of room for expansion. You've talked about enlarging—so this would be a good time to get it done. I really think it's best."

Kate shrugged in defeat. "All right. Draw up the plans and send me the bill." So much for a crowded living space pushing them together. The forced intimacy would have helped—now she'd have to think of something else.

Dylan looked scandalized. "I couldn't do that."

"Why not? It's just like the last time."

"Like hell. Husbands don't charge their wives for work they do."

Much as Kate enjoyed the oblique reference to being Dylan's wife, she didn't think it was right for him to work on the converted carriage house without getting paid.

"That isn't fair," she objected.

"Tough," he said, still sounding offended. "You won't change my mind on this, Katydid. As a matter of fact, you'll have to get used to not getting your way on everything. I'm not spending the next year saying 'yes' to you."

He set his jaw, looking so endearingly macho and stubborn that a quiver went through her stomach. There'd always been a core of strength and certainty in Dylan that fascinated her. He was like a giant boulder in the middle of a river that water had no choice but to flow around. No matter what he might say, she'd never been able to talk him into anything that he didn't actually want to do.

"Do you understand, Katydid?" he said insistently.

Her chin rose. "I understand. I'm not as spoiled as you think, and that's something *you'll* have to get used to."

The level note in Kate's voice made Dylan's eyes narrow. He had the uncomfortable feeling he'd missed something significant, but he didn't know what. Hell, women were a complete mystery. If he didn't comprehend his own sisters, what made him think a woman like Katrina Douglas would be any easier? She lived in an ivory tower, and he lived in the real world.

"I just…all right," he said finally. "When do you want to…uh…?"

"Get married?"

The easy way she said "married" made him wince. At least it was only for a year, and he wouldn't have to feel responsible for her getting hooked up with the wrong man. Anyway, taking care of Kate was such a habit he wasn't sure how to stop.

"Yeah, married," Dylan muttered.

"It needs to be before my birthday, that's all."

"Okay, the sooner we do it, the sooner it'll be over with. We don't have to do one of those big society weddings do we?" he asked. "Your grandmother didn't make *that* a requirement, did she?"

"No, just that I get married and live with my husband on the Douglas estate."

"I'm surprised she put something so specific in the will."

"I'm not," Kate said glumly. "Grandmamma might

have been old, but she had a mind like a steel trap. She was probably suspicious that I'd try to get around the conditions of my inheritance."

Dylan's breath caught in his throat as Kate stretched slowly, arching her back like a silky little cat. She took her time, reaching her hands toward the ceiling, her body twisting sensuously. It was totally innocent, and totally devastating to his already shaky peace of mind.

When she lowered her arms again she smiled lazily. "Sorry. I haven't been sleeping well with so much to think about. It'll be better tonight now that we're getting things settled."

Great.

She was going to sleep like a baby, and he was going home to a cold shower.

Gritting his teeth, Dylan ordered his body to stop behaving like a teenager with his first case of lust. This was *Katydid,* for heaven's sake, he didn't have any business getting stirred up over her. She'd asked for his help because she trusted him. Besides, it was temporary insanity. He'd get over it and then everything would be the same between them.

Ignoring the voice inside his brain that was laughing sarcastically, he leaned forward.

"How do you want to handle the ceremony?"

Kate drew a circle on the table with the tip of her finger. "How about going over to Victoria? Your brother's wedding there was beautiful."

A frown creased Dylan's forehead. Victoria, British Columbia, was popular with courting couples, and the O'Rourke women had raved endlessly over what a romantic setting it had been for Kane and Beth's wedding.

But it didn't seem right for him to marry Katydid in a place intended for lovers, not when they were just friends making a paper commitment for a year. It was much easier thinking about it that way—a paper commitment. Not really a marriage.

"I'd rather keep it smaller, here in Seattle," he said after a moment. "Maybe just the two of us in a civil ceremony at the courthouse."

Kate's eyelids dropped instantly, yet he thought he saw disappointment in their sea-green depths before it was hidden. But surely she didn't want a romantic wedding—or worse, a church wedding. There was something sacrilegious about going into a church and promising to love, honor and cherish when you were planning to get divorced in a year.

"Won't your mother be disappointed?" Kate murmured after a moment. "I know how much she enjoyed it when Kane and the others got married. We could ask her pastor to do the ceremony. It wouldn't have to be a big deal."

Dylan winced.

Much as he wanted his mother to stop pestering him about settling down, he didn't want to hurt her. But she'd be both worried and appalled if she knew the truth about *why* he was marrying Katydid. Fond as she was of Kate, she'd say they were making a huge mistake by using the sacred institution of marriage for something other than love. He was a little uneasy about it himself, but it wasn't as if they'd *really* be married.

No sex, for one thing.

Lord, the next year was going to be dismal.

Unfortunately, sex deprivation didn't seem like a

good enough reason to say no. Dylan cleared his throat. Kate was so innocent, she probably didn't have a clue about what she was asking from him.

"Katydid...I just don't feel comfortable about having some preacher speak words over us." His inexplicable physical reaction to her was causing another kind of discomfort, but she didn't need to know about *that*.

A stillness crept over Kate until she slowly nodded. "I see. So we'll do it at a courthouse, or wherever civil ceremonies are offered."

Swell, now he felt like a selfish crumb.

Husbands probably felt like that a lot, so he was getting off to a good start. Moreover, it didn't even make sense because Kate knew the ceremony wasn't supposed to mean anything. So why did he feel guilty?

He sighed. "Look, I know you wanted—"

"No," she interrupted quietly. "You don't know. It's fine. We'll have a civil ceremony and explain that we were in too much of a hurry to wait for a big wedding. That should satisfy the lawyers. They've been nagging me about the deadline, anyway, so they should understand."

Dylan searched Kate's face, trying to guess what was going through her head. If she thought anyone would understand their marriage, then she was fooling herself. Katydid was like a shaft of moonlight—beautiful and unattainable, with quicksilver emotions and a pedigree of snobbish old wealth and privilege. While he was the son of down-to-earth Irish immigrants who'd worked hard and made a place for themselves in a new country.

They were utterly incompatible.

The only reason anyone might be deceived was because of the charity events she'd dragged him to over the years. Of course, his family had often hinted about something between them, but he'd always laughed it off.

Now they were the ones who'd be laughing.

Chapter Three

"Hold on for a minute," Kane O'Rourke ordered.

Dylan wanted to yank his collar open, but his brother was too busy fastening the tie around his neck. Kane had filled their father's shoes after his death, and he seemed to think this was one of his responsibilities.

"I can't breathe," Dylan grumbled.

"The groom has to be presentable, and that means a properly tied tie. Isn't that right?" Kane appealed to the rest of the male O'Rourkes crowded into the smallest of their mother's upstairs bedrooms.

The others nodded agreement with varying shades of amusement on their faces.

Dylan's carefully laid plans for a quiet civil ceremony at the courthouse hadn't materialized. Instead he was marrying Kate in his mother's backyard with the entire family—plus a few dozen uncles, aunts and cousins—in attendance.

"I feel like a damn fool," Dylan muttered.

"It's the O'Rourke curse," Neil said mildly. "Remember? Putting women and O'Rourke men together usually results in the men feeling foolish."

A chorus of agreement followed, making Dylan glare. They didn't know the half of it. And what did Neil know about it anyway? Or Kane and Patrick? They were besotted over their wives. He'd never seen more billing and cooing in his life than when the three couples were together at family gatherings.

Now *he* was supposedly joining the ranks of happily-in-love-and-delighted-to-be-married.

With an effort Dylan unclenched his jaw. His sisters-in-law were a charming trio of women, but ever since he'd announced his engagement to Kate, things had gotten completely out of control. You would have thought he planned to have the ceremony in an alligator-infested swamp rather than a courthouse.

What was wrong with a courthouse? A simple civil ceremony, no witnesses required—it was the best way to get married, especially when you didn't really plan to *be* married. But that was the problem—he couldn't admit any such thing.

"I suppose everyone thinks I'm going to be next," said Connor with a grim look on his face. He was the youngest of the brothers, twenty-seven, and even more determinedly single than the rest of them. That is, the way the rest of them *used* to be.

Just wait a year, little brother, Dylan advised silently. *I'll be rejoining the bachelor ranks.*

Well, it might be over a year.

He'd been thinking that it wouldn't look good to the

lawyers if he dumped Kate on her cute rear end after twelve months. They should go a while longer so it wouldn't seem quite so much as if she'd gotten married just for her grandmother's house. It might not make any difference legally, but he didn't want Kate to be embarrassed. There'd been so much hysteria over putting the wedding together that he hadn't had time to tell her.

A knock came at the door. "Is everyone decent in there? And fully clothed?" called their mother's voice.

Everyone except Connor chuckled. It was an old joke, going back to the time when the preacher had come to visit on a hot Sunday afternoon and six-year-old Connor had streaked through the house, bare-butt naked. When Pegeen had scolded her son, he'd looked at her earnestly and said he *was* decent because he'd just been to church, but that it was so much cooler without clothing.

"I wish everyone would just forget about that," Connor grumbled. Being the youngest son wasn't easy, but it was an old complaint and lacked any heat.

Patrick reached out to open the door, a smile still on his face. "Decent *and* clothed," he said.

"All right, then. Now all of you go on downstairs, I want to talk with Dylan." Her Irish brogue was stronger than usual, the way it always was when she was feeling emotional.

Dylan watched his brothers and two closest cousins file good-naturedly from the room. He knew his mother had spoken privately with Kane, Patrick and Neil before their weddings, and he'd been dreading the moment; lying didn't come easily, particularly to someone he loved.

Pegeen hesitated, then sighed softly. "Your father always wanted to be here, talkin' to you before you got married. But then, I think you know what he'd say, don't you?"

"I know."

Keenan O'Rourke had taught his sons simple lessons about honor and fidelity and about what being a man meant; lessons that were part of the everyday fabric of living and not just for special occasions. So, yes, Dylan knew what his father would say. The words weren't necessary.

"It's a fine thing to make your own way in the world," Pegeen murmured. "And you're a fine man. But pay heed to what your heart tells you, son. 'Tis the one thing you've forgotten how to do."

A frown creased Dylan's forehead, but his mother continued before he could say anything.

"Only I shan't worry overmuch," she said. "Your Katydid is a darling child. She'll help you to listen to your heart, as well as your head."

"She's a child, all right," Dylan agreed without thinking, then winced. He hardly sounded like an adoring groom. "That is, she's still so young."

A smile curved his mother's lips, reminding him of a cat with cream on its whiskers. "You've never wanted to see her as grown up, but she's old enough to know what she wants. Katrina has a woman's needs. I don't think she'll be lettin' you forget that."

He got a peculiar feeling, rather like the ground was moving beneath him in an earthquake. The whole conversation was making him uneasy—much like his recent discussions with Kate. She was honest and straightforward about everything, and yet he kept sensing currents of unspoken emotions. He supposed it was natural, she'd once had dreams of love and happily-ever-after, and here she was, forced to get married because of her battle-ax of a grandmother. Or rather, because of the battle-ax's last will and testament.

He'd had his own lawyer look at the will, and Jane Douglas had indeed tied up her estate in language as stern and unbreakable as she'd once been herself.

The stubborn old bat.

"Is it time to go downstairs?" he asked gruffly.

"I'll send one of the boys up when Kate is ready," Pegeen assured. She kissed him, then paused at the door. "'Tis bad luck to see the bride before the wedding."

Dylan closed his eyes and restrained his groan. What would his mother say about "luck" when he ended up with a divorce in a little over a year? He couldn't tell anyone it was really like an annulment since they wouldn't be intimate. One thing was clear from the will, it had to *appear* to be a real marriage, even if it wasn't.

Maybe they could just say they'd mistaken friendship for love and had decided to end things before they made each other miserable. It sounded okay but Dylan still didn't feel right about it.

Lord, Katydid had gotten him into some messes before, but this one was a doozy.

The strains of the wedding march spilled through the garden and Kate held her breath. Her heart was pounding so hard she was shaking from her white satin shoes to the miniature roses pinned in her hair.

She knew Dylan wasn't happy about how the quiet courthouse ceremony had become a romantic garden affair, but it was the wedding she'd always dreamed of having. And, since she expected it to be her one and *only* wedding, it was fine with her, even if he was upset about it.

"Ready?" asked Kane O'Rourke. He smiled and extended his arm. "I'm sorry your parents couldn't be here, but I'm honored to fill in as 'father of the bride.'"

"I'm the one who's honored," Kate said sincerely, yet a stab of guilt went through her. She hadn't wanted to hear her parents disparage Dylan, so she'd waited until the last minute before calling them in London to say she was getting married. Her father had missed so many of the important events in her life, it never occurred to her that he'd be disappointed not to walk her down the aisle.

It had never occurred to her that they'd want to come at all.

She searched Kane's face, wondering if he disapproved of the hasty way his brother was getting married. If he did, he hadn't said so. The O'Rourkes had been so supportive it made her want to cry. Was love supposed to be this difficult?

"It's time to go," he said. "Ready?"

"As ready as I'll ever be." But they hadn't taken three steps before her feet faltered. "You know how much I love Dylan, don't you?"

"I think the whole family knows that."

Everyone except Dylan, Kate thought to herself. She forced herself to breathe. "I'll do everything possible to make him happy," she said.

"Well, if my little brother gives you trouble, you've got my number. It's about time he woke up when it comes to you."

She blinked and walked out of the house with Kane, at the same time thinking about what he'd said.

It's about time he woke up when it comes to you...

Did Kane know that Dylan wasn't in love with her? Maybe he thought Dylan really *was* in love, but hadn't realized it yet. Or Kane might be deluding himself, just wanting to believe his brother had fallen in love.

Maybe...she dragged her racing thoughts under control. Maybe it didn't mean anything.

It was a lovely day, unusually warm for May in the Seattle area, and the yard was filled with flowers, both growing and arranged in baskets set in every available space. Kate might have wanted a romantic wedding, but she'd tried to support Dylan's plans for a courthouse ceremony. As a result his mother and the rest of the family had taken over. The place was beautiful. The photographer Pegeen had hired would be pleased.

Dylan waited for her in front of a rose-covered arbor, banked in ferns. His face was impassive, almost cold, and she shivered. The idea that she might be making a huge mistake was foremost in her mind. But Dylan wasn't cold like her father, he was a decent, wonderful man, even if he did look as remote as an Alaskan glacier at the moment.

Just then he smiled and her heart melted. For once in her life she was going to take the risk of getting what she really wanted, and she'd deal with the doubts later.

"Hey, there, Katydid," he murmured, holding out his hand.

She wasn't wearing gloves and the hard calluses on Dylan's fingers against her softer skin sent sensual images through her mind. What would it be like to have those same calloused fingers caressing her body? Would she ever find out?

Warmth crept up Kate's face, and she hastily focused her attention on the judge's face. One thing Dylan had succeeded on having was a civil, rather than religious, ceremony. She'd tried not to let it hurt, knowing Dylan saw the whole thing as just a favor to her, but she would have liked having Pegeen's pastor do the wedding.

The judge said a few words about the sanctity of marriage and Dylan stiffened. Her tummy, already swooping with nerves, took a plunge that rivaled the highest roller coaster drop in the world. How would she get him to look at her in a whole new way if he was so against it in the first place? It wasn't a new thought, it just seemed more of a problem now that they were actually *getting* married.

"Do you, Dylan James O'Rourke, take this woman to be your lawfully wedded wife?" asked the judge.

"I do," he replied.

"Do you, Katrina Cecelia Douglas, take this man to be your lawfully wedded husband?" asked the judge.

"I...do."

Her slight hesitation earned a quick glance from Dylan, who had been staring at the hedge. One of his eyebrows lifted. He wouldn't back down now, not having promised to help her, but he undoubtedly hoped that *she'd* decided she couldn't go through with it. The judge, a friend of the O'Rourkes, continued smoothly, seeming unaware of the undercurrents between bride and groom.

Dylan looked positively fierce when he had to repeat the vow to "love, honor and cherish." Luckily the moment passed before anyone noticed, and she was making the same promise.

The wedding band slid over Kate's third finger, sending another pang of regret through her. Dylan wouldn't be wearing a ring himself, he'd told the family it wouldn't be safe with him working with construction equipment. She was the only one who knew it was just an excuse, one more reminder of their temporary arrangement.

When the judge said it was time for them to kiss, Kate's lungs refused to function. How often had she dreamed of kissing Dylan, only to wake up and find it wasn't real? Friendly hugs and busses on the cheek weren't the same as the way a man embraces a woman.

Dylan put his hands on her shoulders and drew her close. Their gazes locked, then he looked down and focused on her mouth. Could he see the pulse jumping in her throat, the heat blooming across her skin, just because he was close?

Dylan, Kate cried silently. She'd give him anything he wanted, if she just knew what it was.

Very gently, he pressed a polite kiss to her mouth and ice condensed around her stomach. She couldn't bear the thought of him drawing back, still so cool and remote, and she opened her mouth to protest.

This is our wedding, please...

Dylan felt Kate's rush of breath and without conscious thought pulled her against him. She was clean and fresh, and he deepened the kiss, forgetting that she was the kid he'd always taken care of.

Sweet...she tasted so sweet.

He thrust his tongue between her teeth, trying to capture the elusive flavor, his senses infused with her fragrant warmth. He hadn't held anything so soft in longer than he could remember, and his blood burned hot and heavy in his groin. She arched against him, her breasts seeming to plump into his chest. A ringing sound filled his ears.

This was *Kate,* not a woman like…well, other women.

Coming to the realization he'd French-kissed her in front of his family and friends, Dylan lifted his head. She blinked at him, looking as shocked as he felt. And why not? They were supposed to be playacting.

Yet his body didn't seem to know it was an act. His body wanted a wedding night like a normal groom.

"I would like to present Mr. and Mrs. O'Rourke," the judge announced.

The O'Rourkes surged forward, excited and congratulating them with kisses for Kate and pleased hugs and slaps on the back for Dylan, smoothing over the moment.

Kate trembled and tried to think straight. Dylan's passionate kiss should have delighted her, but he had a fixed smile on his face and wouldn't look at her. Tears pooled in her eyes. Fortunately everyone assumed she was simply happy and emotional. Brides were supposed to cry, weren't they? Nobody needed to know her heart was breaking.

"I'm so delighted for you," Beth O'Rourke said. She gave Kate an awkward hug, impeded by being nine months pregnant.

"Sweetheart, you know the doctor told you to keep off your feet," Kane scolded, tucking an arm around his wife and leaning forward to kiss Kate. "My brother is a lucky man, Katrina."

"I'm getting a complex," Dylan complained. "Everyone keeps telling me how fortunate I am. Doesn't anyone think Kate is lucky, too?"

"Of course she's fortunate," Pegeen said with a mother's staunch loyalty. "And she's such a lovely bride."

"Very lovely," Dylan agreed, casting a quick glance at the bride in question.

Kate looked like an angel in her white lace dress and gold hair, crowned with tiny roses. If she didn't have the sparkle that Beth and his other sisters-in-law had worn at their weddings, then he was probably the only one who'd noticed.

A twinge of guilt hit, but he didn't have any reason to feel guilty, dammit—he was the one helping her out, not the other way around.

It was just like the other crazy schemes she'd talked him into when they were kids. He remembered the first day his father had brought him along to the Douglas estate. Keenan had considered the long drive into Seattle to be worth the effort since the Douglases paid so well, and he'd arranged to bring one or more of his sons along to help.

Dylan smiled. They'd helped all right, but the real reason they'd gone was to spend time with their dad.

So they'd driven inside—through the rear gate of course—and little Katydid had dashed out to greet them, cute as a china doll with big green eyes and long golden curls. She'd looked at him, ducked her head, then shot him a shy smile that went straight through his boyish heart. For a long time after that he'd been her willing slave.

The sound of a spoon tapping on a glass pulled Dylan's attention back to the present. It was Kane, who'd been dividing his attention between his very pregnant wife and his duties as the eldest brother.

"Ladies and gentlemen," Kane said, smiling across the assembled O'Rourkes and related families. "A year ago Pegeen O'Rourke had only two fine granddaughters, despite being the mother of nine grown children. She couldn't understand our stubbornness about getting married and providing her with a whole new generation of grandkids to teach her Irish brogue."

Chuckles rose from the crowd and Dylan saw Patrick fold his arms around Maddie, who was five months pregnant herself.

Dylan was pretty certain his sister-in-law, Libby, wasn't expecting yet, but Libby and Neil were busy running a new division of Kane's company. They didn't have time for babies.

So, what excuse could he manufacture for him and Kate to delay starting a family? His business was going well, and Kate wasn't a career woman. Considering their haste in getting married, people would probably think she was pregnant already. He could imagine the snide comments she'd have to endure from her society friends until it was obvious she hadn't married because of an unplanned pregnancy. Then they'd just be snide because of her construction worker husband.

Kate didn't deserve that.

She was bright and open, and as elusive as a swallowtail butterfly dancing on the breeze, but she wasn't a snob.

"With this joyous ceremony, Pegeen now finds herself with four daughters-in-law," Kane continued, "and with two more grandbabies on the way, she's—"

A faint gasp from Beth drew Kane's attention, but she smiled and shook her head when he took a step toward her.

"Er…yes," he went on, his gaze fixed on his wife. "Needless to say, she's extremely happy a fourth son has finally had the good sense to get married. Isn't that right, mother?"

"Aye. Now if only m'daughters would be so cooperative," Pegeen said, smiling. "And my youngest son, of course."

A collective laugh came from the guests, while the daughters in question made faces.

A hand crept into Dylan's, and he knew it belonged to Kate. Since it was only appropriate for the bride and groom to stand next to each other during the bridal toast, he laced their fingers together, trying not to think about their kiss.

It had shocked him.

How could he have responded to Katydid like that? She was beautiful, but they were friends, not lovers. Technically she might have just become his wife, but it was only a legal agreement they would end in a year. It had become a litany in his head—Kate wouldn't be a real wife, so it wasn't a real marriage.

Period.

Thinking any other way would drive him crazy.

Kane raised his glass along with the others. "So please join me in welcoming Katrina Douglas O'Rourke to our family. Dylan, Kate, may you have a long and happy life together."

"And many, many children," Pegeen added.

A chorus of agreement and the clinking of glasses followed the toast. Dylan looked down and saw Katydid's strained smile. It probably mirrored his own, though it wasn't the first time since he'd agreed to marry her that he'd wondered exactly what she was thinking.

A sudden yelp brought a welcome interruption. Beth was bent over, supported by Kane, who had a wild, glazed expression in his eyes.

"She's in labor. Call an ambulance," he shouted.

"No," Beth said, straightening as the contraction eased. "First babies take longer, don't they, Mom?"

Pegeen nodded to her daughter-in-law. "'Tis right. But when did the contractions start, darlin'?"

Beth blew out a breath. "During the ceremony. I had some twinges last night that made me wonder, but I'm sure it—"

"Why didn't you say something?" Kane demanded.

She patted his arm. "Because you would have over-reacted and I wanted to come to the wedding. Besides, if the baby starts to come, I'm sure Connor can help out."

"Connor is a veterinarian! You aren't having kittens."

Despite his inner turmoil, Dylan enjoyed the frantic look on his brother's face. Kane was usually so unflappable…about everything except his wife. When it came to Beth, Kane was so wildly in love that he was completely irrational.

"I think an M.D. would be best under the circumstances," said Liam O'Rourke, a cousin Dylan didn't know well. He was a practicing physician who'd recently moved back to the Seattle area from Chicago. "Let's go inside and I'll give Beth a quick exam."

Beth sent Kate an apologetic look. "I'm so sorry to interfere with your big day."

"Don't be silly," Kate assured her. "I can't imagine anything better. It makes the whole thing more memorable."

"Everyone stay and enjoy the party. We'll be back out in a minute," Beth said. "I'm not going to miss this reception."

"Unless you're giving birth," muttered Kane.

With the mood broken, everyone began drifting around, helping themselves to food and catching up on news. Kate ditched her wedding bouquet behind a rhododendron bush and began serving cake. There were a few protests about getting pictures of the bride and groom and the traditional cake cutting ceremony, but she just shook her head and kept filling plates.

Anything to keep from crying.

Why in the world, now that she was halfway to getting what she wanted, was she so sad?

She'd *known* Dylan didn't want a wedding that smacked of a real marriage and commitment. And while she'd been secretly thrilled with the romantic frills and mood of the day, she now realized how false it all was. There was nothing romantic about her arrangement with Dylan, and Beth going into labor was just another reminder that his name on a marriage certificate didn't mean anything.

Kane adored Beth, while Dylan saw her as an overindulged kid who needed rescuing on a regular basis.

She had a year to make things work between them, and until then, she wouldn't be a member of the O'Rourke family, no matter how many wedding toasts were made or how warmly they welcomed her.

"Are you okay?" Dylan asked a few minutes later, when she'd finally been coaxed away from the cake table and was sitting with a plate of food on her lap.

"I'm fine."

"You look pale."

"I'm always pale."

He raised a skeptical eyebrow. "You also aren't eating."

"I'm not hungry. You eat it," Kate muttered, handing him the plate. Her stomach was unsettled enough.

With a small shrug, Dylan dug his fork into the food. *His* appetite certainly didn't seem affected, she thought irritably. Why was he so stubborn? Why did he keep seeing her as a child, rather than a grown woman? She felt frozen in time when it came to Dylan, as if caught in an ageless piece of amber. If she had any sense she would have given up years ago.

But at least she would finally know if there was any hope for them. If the worst happened, she wouldn't stay in the Seattle area. There were too many reminders of the past here, too much chance of being caught unaware by emotions and old hurts. And by memories. Some memories would haunt her forever, like being kissed by Dylan and the stormy expression on his face afterward.

If he hadn't wanted to kiss her like that, why had he done it?

They were alone for the moment and she took a breath. "Dylan, about earlier, when you…we…"

"I know, Mom must be ecstatic with the baby coming," he said, deliberately misunderstanding. She sighed. Men in general avoided discussing relationships, why should Dylan be an exception?

A hand tugged on her skirt and she looked down. It was either Amy or Peggy, though she didn't know which one was which. Amy and Peggy were Pegeen's identical twin granddaughters.

"Are you my aunt now?" the child asked.

"Y…yes."

"Goody." She clambered into Kate's lap and kissed her.

Kate's spirits lifted. She could never be sad around children who were healthy and happy.

"Amy 'n' me are having a cousin," the youngster announced.

Amy. That meant this was Peggy.

"Yes, Peggy, you'll have a cousin before you know it," Kate said. She stood and balanced the four-year-old on her hip. If she was very lucky, she might be holding her own child in a year or two. With Dylan as the father.

"Goodness, she's far too heavy for you," Kathleen called. She rushed over and put out her arms.

"We're fine."

"Better let her," Shannon O'Rourke suggested. "Sooner or later you're going to have to throw the bouquet, and there are lots of single ladies here hoping to catch it."

Kate swallowed and reluctantly let go of Peggy. "My flowers? Heavens, I've lost track of them."

Shannon lifted an eyebrow. "I'll organize a search. We wouldn't want to disappoint anyone. Several of the cousins are getting anxious."

"Hah. You're the one who's secretly hoping to catch the bouquet," Dylan said.

His sister sent him a warning glance. "One wedding this summer is enough. Besides, I'm not the least bit domestic."

"You can say that again."

An unreadable emotion flickered in Shannon's eyes before she tossed her head. "Why would I say it a second time, when my family is more than willing to point it out on every occasion?"

His forehead creased in confusion, and Kate dug her elbow into his side. Honestly, men were so dense.

Dylan looked down at Kate. "What?"

"Don't you have something to do?" she asked sweetly.

He looked at her warily. "Such as?"

Jumping off a cliff sounded like a good idea at the moment, but she'd probably regret it if he did.

In a day or so.

"You could check on how Kane is surviving," she suggested.

"Uh…right. I'll be back." Dylan beat a hasty retreat.

"I should hope so—you wouldn't want to miss the honeymoon," Shannon called after him.

Dylan turned slowly. "We're not going on a honeymoon. Summers are busy for contractors, and Katydid has a number of charity events she's committed to. We'll go later."

Shannon frowned, then stuck out her tongue as her brother disappeared into the house.

"No honeymoon?" she asked.

"Uh…maybe later," Kate said lamely.

She'd suggested they go away, at least for a long weekend, but Dylan had refused. It was just like her idea of getting married in Victoria or having a preacher. He didn't want it to seem like a marriage at all. A honeymoon, even a fake one, was out of the question.

"A honeymoon is half the fun of getting hitched."

"We'll honeymoon—on weekends, evenings after we're finished…that is, after Dylan is finished working."

Shannon didn't seem convinced. "But why not go now?"

Kate crossed her fingers behind her back. "It's a bad time, like Dylan said, but I had this superstition about getting married before my birthday. He was sweet and went along with me, even though it would have been better to wait."

"All right, but you don't know what you're missing."

Kate slumped into a chair as her new sister-in-law strolled away, calling to everyone to look for the bridal bouquet.

"I know what I'm missing," she mumbled, thinking about Dylan's broad shoulders and strong body—a body that wouldn't be crawling under her sheets anytime soon. A frustrated ache sank low into her abdomen. "I know exactly what I'm missing."

Dylan noticed Kate was silent the entire drive into Seattle. When they arrived at the converted carriage house, she jumped out and opened the front door while he was getting his suitcases from the back of his truck. She was already shoving leftover wedding cake into the freezer when he walked inside.

"I don't know why Mom insisted on sending that home with us," he muttered.

"It's the top layer," Katydid said as if that explained everything. She put the rest of the food—some of the reception leftovers—into the refrigerator.

"So?"

"So it's traditional to eat the top layer on the first anniversary. That's why it isn't cut at the reception. Your mother wrapped it very carefully to be sure it would keep."

"Oh."

Dylan had never paid much attention to wedding traditions, but it stood to reason that Katydid would know. He remembered her as a little girl, dressing up as a bride and begging him to play the groom. Until now he'd always refused—even as a child he'd never envisioned marrying a spoiled princess. The idea that he was now legally wed to the Douglas family heiress—the most spoiled princess of them all—was a little more than he could comprehend.

"It's great about Kane and Beth's baby," he said uncomfortably. "A girl. Kane is so proud I think he burst all the buttons on his shirt."

"I suppose you'd want a son."

"I don't want either."

Kate looked appalled. "You don't want children?"

"Maybe someday, but we have the next year to survive before I can think about that."

Hurt filled her eyes and Dylan groaned. Things were harder now, awkward in a way they'd never been between them.

"Yes, well…are you sure you don't want the large bedroom?" she asked.

The change of subject startled him, though it shouldn't have. Their wedding had put an end to Kate's dreams of love everlasting and family and babies. Maybe she'd feel better if she understood it wasn't an end to those dreams, just a postponement. After they were divorced she could get married again and have a grand bash to put their garden ceremony to shame.

"Katydid…I realize this has been hard for you," Dylan said slowly. He might not be happy about getting talked into her scheme, but he still cared about her.

"You don't need to worry about me."

"I do worry. You haven't been yourself all day. I know you've had ideas about love and everything going along with it, and your grandmother screwed that up. But it isn't forever. You'll be able to get back to doing whatever you want."

"I see."

When she didn't say anything else, he shifted uneasily. "Well, I'm going to grab a shower and pull out some work. I'm putting together a proposal for the J.R. Hansmeir Building. Unless you want to shower first...?"

"No, I'm going to read for a while."

Kate waited until Dylan was in the bathroom, with the water running. She sighed and glanced around her cozy little home.

Dylan already had the plans drawn up to enlarge the carriage house living area, adding a second bathroom, a combination office and den, and another bedroom on the opposite end from hers. A bedroom he planned to use once his construction crew was done. She was surprised he hadn't planned separate entrances or decided to build an entirely separate apartment.

"I wish you knew what I want, Dylan," Kate said softly. "I really do."

She curled up on the couch and lifted her novel. It was a tale of two lovers in medieval England, trapped by circumstances beyond their control. But tonight of all nights, it had no hope of holding her attention and after a while she put her head down on the cushion, staring into the empty fireplace. Here she was, sitting alone on her wedding night.

A tear dripped down her cheek.

This was really pathetic.

A second tear joined the first.

She could be honest with Dylan and explain everything, but that would send him running for the door so fast he'd be a blur on the way out. And on top of everything else she felt dreadful for the way she'd deceived him.

The tears began falling so fast she couldn't count them, and after a couple minutes she fled into her room.

Chapter Four

Dylan stood in the shower and let cool water stream over him, wishing it could wash away memories of everything that had happened that day. But a river of ice water couldn't make him forget the heated moment in the garden when he'd kissed his bride.

"It was just one of those freak things," he muttered, sticking his head under the spray. "I must have been out of my mind. It could never happen again," he added, standing straight again and slicking water from his hair.

He didn't want Kate, not like that. They were friends and he felt responsible for her because she'd been part of his life for so long, but that was all.

Shaking his head, Dylan turned off the water. The awkwardness of living with another person struck him as he reached for a towel—he hadn't thought to bring a robe into the bathroom. He'd have to put his clothes back on, just to reach the bedroom without embarrassing Kate. For an instant he wondered how much experience she actually *had* seeing men in their altogether, but it wasn't any of his business, no matter what sort of legal tangle they'd gotten themselves into.

The sound of hurrying footsteps came down the short hallway, then a door opened and closed.

Kate.

Dylan dried himself, hitched the thick towel around his hips and cracked the door.

"Kate?"

She didn't answer right away.

"Katydid?" he prompted again.

"Yes?" Her reply sounded muffled and Dylan frowned.

"Are you staying put for a couple minutes?"

"Uh…sure. Wha-whatever you…w-want."

Damn.

Dylan had enough experience with four sisters to know when a girl was crying and trying not to let it show. He'd rather have hit his foot with a sledgehammer than talk to her about it, but he strode to the bedroom and donned the robe he'd bought after agreeing to Kate's not-so-convenient marriage plan, then headed back to her door.

"What's wrong, Katydid?" he called softly.

There was another long silence, then he heard the barely discernable sound of a sniff. "N-nothing."

Oh, yeah.

He believed that.

Being sensitive and a great listener wasn't his forte, but even if he didn't consider that marriage ceremony to be real, Kate was sort of his…wife.

Wife.

His gut churned as he turned her bedroom doorknob. He'd never wanted this kind of responsibility or involvement, but here he was, regardless.

When he walked inside, Kate bolted upright and hastily wiped her cheeks. His stomach twisted again; those weren't the crocodile tears she'd used when they were kids to sucker him into her schemes, she was genuinely upset and didn't want him to see. It was just like when her grandmother had died, and she'd pretended it was all right. Kate's heart could be breaking and she'd try to keep anyone from knowing.

Anyone?

Even him?

Dylan's equilibrium took an unpleasant jolt. He'd never thought of it that way before, but it might be true. Most of the time he didn't have a clue what Kate was thinking and feeling. He ought not to mind, preferring privacy himself, but for some reason it bothered him— before he would have sworn she was as open to him as a yellow-eyed daisy.

"Hey, Kate," he murmured.

She promptly turned her back on him, shoulders quivering. "I'm fine. Go away."

His instincts shouted at him, saying to leave it alone, to let her work out whatever problem was making her sad. It might not even be a real problem, but melancholy or that time of the month. Of course, if he suggested any such thing it would just confirm that he was a crude male pig with the sensitivity of a brick wall. But even as Dylan decided it was okay and he didn't mind being branded a male pig, her shoulders quivered once more.

Hellfire.

"It's okay, Katydid, honest," he said helplessly. "It's going to work out. We won't let the lawyers win or anything, and you can marry someone else someday."

Kate's stomach heaved.

Marry someone else?

She knew Dylan didn't mean to make her feel worse, but every time he opened his mouth, it was like acid pouring on her aching conscience. She wanted *Dylan*, not someone else. And she hated hearing him reassure her about another marriage that wasn't ever going to happen. Loving Dylan and wanting to be with him wasn't going to change; her heart and soul weren't made that way.

"You don't have to worry about it. Go work on your proposal for that new building complex," she muttered, straightening her shoulders. As long as he didn't come around the bed and see the tears still dripping down her cheeks, he wouldn't be any the wiser.

"No. You're upset."

Drat him. Kate gritted her teeth. He was stubborn and impossible and she loved him to distraction. "I'll bet you think it's just hormones."

She shot him a surreptitious glance and saw a guilty look flash across his handsome, rugged features.

"I didn't say that," he muttered.

She choked back a sob.

Maybe it *was* hormones. She wasn't the kind of woman who cried at the drop of a hat, weepy over wobbly kittens and sentimental television commercials. It was ironic that Dylan thought she was a sheltered, immature child when she'd learned to be independent and take care of herself. She didn't have much choice—her family wasn't exactly the emotionally supportive type, any more than Dylan had ever...

She swallowed.

No.

She wasn't going to compare Dylan to her family. He was a great guy, even if he'd seemed like a stranger all day.

The mattress dipped as he sat next to her.

"I suppose that's the sort of thing you'd expect from a construction worker like me," Dylan said quietly. "Something sarcastic about hormones."

"No, but you're a guy." Kate gave in and leaned against him, her cheek landing in the hollow of his shoulder. "I doubt guys can help thinking stuff like that, only the nice ones don't say it."

"That's me, a nice construction worker," Dylan said wryly.

"I'm talking about all men, and you're the best man I know, so stop being so hung up on that construction worker stuff. You're strong and honest and...and..." Her breathing got ragged, and she sniffed.

"Oh, God, don't start again." Dylan put an arm around her and stroked her hair. "I'm sure it'll be better tomorrow."

Kate tried to stop her tears. She'd promised herself there wouldn't be any tricks or games in their marriage; if Dylan chose to stay with her, it would be because he truly loved her.

She angled her head back. "Are you really upset about being here? Because if you are..." She choked.

"Jeez." Dylan pulled Kate across his lap, feeling desperate. It was strange, wanting to comfort her, at the same time wishing he was on a different planet. "It's all right," he whispered. "I'd rather be here than see you married to someone you don't want to be with."

"Really?"

"I mean what I say. You know that."

"I know."

She let out a shuddering sigh, snuggling closer, and his body hardened—holding Kate was a big mistake. A *huge* mistake. He drew a deep breath, which was another mistake because she smelled like a garden of flowers. The hell of it was that she hadn't done a thing to warrant his reacting to her, but the warmth of her breath on his throat and her slight weight across his thighs were playing the devil with his restraint.

He'd never had those kind of feelings for Kate. This was *Kate,* pretty, annoying, bright as a newly minted penny, the kid he'd always protected and taken care of. He socialized with a certain kind of woman, the kind who didn't talk about relationships or expect forever, and she was the complete opposite.

"Are you feeling better now?" he asked, wishing he'd put on a shirt and pair of jeans, instead of a robe. At least they would have helped conceal his response.

"Y-yes."

But a tear dripped onto his chest, through the V-opening of his terry robe, and he groaned.

"Katydid, don't do that."

"I'm sorry. You can leave now. I'm much better."

He searched through swaths of her thick, long gold hair and cupped her chin.

"Look at me," Dylan said firmly, hating the way her lashes swept down, concealing her green eyes.

Truthfully, he didn't quite understand why she was so unhappy. Their marriage represented an inconvenience for the next year, but it wasn't the end of the world. And it had been her idea in the first place.

"I never meant to make things hard for you," she whispered. "It's just a little overwhelming, everything the way it was today, and y-your family being so nice and Kane and Beth's baby coming. And before, when I talked to m-my dad, he said he would have liked to walk me down the aisle. I didn't expect him to feel like that." She hiccuped.

Women were incomprehensible.

"Your father said he wanted to be here?"

"Uh-huh. I didn't think he'd care about it. I really didn't." There was a confused note to Kate's words, which wasn't any wonder. Her father had hardly been present for the important moments in her life. He'd hardly been present in her life, period.

Dylan sighed and leaned down to kiss Kate's forehead. Yet somehow it was her mouth he caught beneath his lips.

A Freudian slip.

An enticing, gut-wrenching slip.

He tasted the salty flavor of tears and found himself deepening the kiss, searching for the sweetness he knew lay below the unhappiness. After a stunned second Kate's arms moved around his waist and neck, and she arched against him.

He groaned, his senses filled with her. She was invigorating, like the tang of evergreen on the breeze, nothing like his usual bed-partners, with their aggressive, bold demands and determination to be responsible for their own sexual fulfillment. He'd applauded that aspect of women's lib, but maybe there was a lot to recommend sharing something…mutual.

Without thinking, Dylan twisted until they were lying on the bed, Kate beneath him. The silky dress she was wearing caught on his rough fingers, but she didn't protest, even when he cupped her breast.

He thrust his tongue deep inside her mouth, forgetting everything but the exploding heat, low in his gut.

"Mmm."

Kate moaned.

Except for dreams about Dylan, she'd never felt anything like the heat streaming through her blood, the tingles sparking deep in her core. She ought to push him away, but she'd waited too long to be held by the man she loved.

So many dreams, waiting to be realized…

Yet all at once she squirmed, realizing this was *nothing* like her dreams. The tense, grabby sensation in her lower abdomen almost hurt, she felt so empty, so needy.

Dylan's thumb rubbed across her nipple, rough and gentle at the same time. She'd changed from her wedding dress into a silk caftan back at Pegeen O'Rourke's house, and the thin, slippery fabric seemed to intensify the hard strength of his touch.

It was like being swept under a tidal wave. Part of her was alarmed, but the part that had waited so long to be held by the man she loved simply let go. Yet enough of her brain was still operating to start rationalizing.

She shouldn't say anything, because it would remind him he was kissing Katydid, not some anonymous woman.

No.

She wasn't anonymous, she wanted him to love *her,* with all his heart and soul.

Still, she'd waited forever to be kissed like this by Dylan. She should just enjoy the moment and let fate take its own path. Unless it would make things more difficult, instead of better, when it came to him falling in love with her.

Dylan, Kate's mind whispered, trying to decide.

He gathered the skirt of her caftan, dragging it up her thigh, and the conflicting mental arguments vanished. Even his skill at shimmying the dress upward didn't distract her, she wanted to be naked even more than she wanted to think about the women he'd held in the past.

He paused at her hip, his finger tracing the narrow band of her silk panties. The grabby sensation below her tummy became impossibly worse, particularly when he massaged the exact spot with his knowing hand.

Her spirits rose, hope welling up in her. Surely this meant that Dylan cared, he seemed so intent on pleasing her.

"Soft," he breathed, as if talking to himself. "I've never felt anything so damned soft."

She threaded her fingers through his hair and tugged him down for another drugging kiss. She loved the taste of him, the endless heat and intoxication.

She'd kissed other men, of course.

After college she'd tried to convince herself that Dylan wasn't the only man on earth, that she was being childish to think he'd fall in love with her after such a long time. So she'd gone out with a number of guys. Problem was, none of them came close to Dylan. She still dated on a casual basis, keeping things light and uncomplicated.

That is…she'd dated until proposing to Dylan.

It was all or nothing now. The culmination of her hopes and dreams, or the worse crash and burn of her life.

All because she'd lied.

Kate's mind instantly shied away from her remorse over deceiving the man she loved.

Concentrate, she ordered.

Dylan cooperated by pressing nibbling kisses down her throat, then teasing her breasts with his hot breath and tickling fingers. Just when the top of her head was ready to blow off from frustration and need, he opened his mouth and drew an aching nipple inside, silk and all.

A startled cry escaped Kate's throat and she arched upward. Moisture and heat instantly soaked through the thin fabric. It was erotic, feeling so much without actually being exposed.

Dylan thought he'd go insane if he didn't have Kate soon. He actually had his hand on the belt of his robe, untying it, before he froze.

Have Kate?

This was *Kate.*

He'd been caressing Kate's breast and kissing her like a crazed, sex-deprived man found living on a desert island.

Little Katydid, who trusted him.

All at once he levered himself from the bed and stared down at her. She looked stunned, and he dragged a breath into his lungs, unable to resist letting his gaze sweep over her slim form. He'd pulled the hem of her dress to her waist, revealing slender legs and gently tapered hips. Her breasts were still covered, but he had no doubt they were just as tantalizing as the rest of her body.

He was appalled.

Sex wasn't why he'd agreed to that wretched ceremony, it was to keep Kate from having to sleep with a man she didn't love in order to get her inheritance.

His hands shook with suppressed emotion as he made sure his robe covered the blatant expression of his desire.

"Kate—"

"Dylan—"

They both spoke at once, and both stopped to let the other have their say. The formal bit of courtesy nearly made him laugh. Right. They were courteous. He'd stomped all over the honor his father and eldest brother had taught him, and now he was being polite. Wasn't that swell of him? He rolled his eyes, more disgusted than ever with himself.

"You go first," Kate said.

She sat up, and in the same smooth motion swept her dress down over her legs. He wasn't sure, but a faint pink seemed to be brightening her cheeks, as if she was self-conscious about being exposed like that.

They were friends, but he'd never even seen her in a swimsuit, much less a pair of skimpy panties. A tube top and shorts were the limit, and even then he'd carefully kept his gaze on her face, instead of her feminine curves. He'd never liked being reminded of how much she'd grown up since those early days when she'd seemed to idolize him.

"I'm sorry. More than I can say. You should have slugged me. God, I can't believe what I just did. It was inexcusable." His jaw clenched.

"You didn't do anything."

"Right. I came in to comfort you, then took advantage. I'm a real prince."

She pushed her hair away from her face, looking uncertain. "Please don't be angry," she whispered.

"I'm angry with myself, not you, Katydid."

"But I don't want you to be angry at all."

Dylan sighed. He didn't know why Kate had singled him out when they were kids, but she had, and he'd be damned before he messed up what feelings she had left for him. Maybe that explained why he'd ultimately said yes to her idea of them getting married for a year—it still made him feel special, knowing how much she trusted him.

"Dylan? Please say something."

"I'm just so sorry," he said. "I promise it won't happen again."

If anything, his second attempt to apologize seemed to make things worse. She attempted a smile, but he recognized that false cheer and knew she was only trying to make him feel better. She only smiled like that when things were so awful she didn't want anyone to know.

"That's all right." Kate smiled again, unintentionally heaping hot coals on his heart. "I don't mind. In fact, I really…" She stopped and shrugged, apparently changing her mind about what she'd planned to say.

"Yeah, well, I'd better get to work on that building proposal."

Kate watched Dylan disappear and thought her heart was tearing right in half.

It hurt more than she could have imagined knowing he regretted touching her. But what else had she expected? It was too soon for them to kiss like that, much less make love. Of course, if she'd been the one to put an end to their kiss, he would have still torn himself apart over that blessed O'Rourke code of honor. She ought to be grateful for his code, but right now she was too frustrated.

Fresh tears slipped down her cheeks, coming from a deep, painful place within. She couldn't go back, only forward, but she was more uncertain now than ever before. Even if Dylan fell in love with her, would it just mean more of the same? Another person she loved who was remote and barely a real part of her life?

The answers weren't available, and Kate finally curled up, holding the memory of Dylan's caresses like a talisman. She'd have to pretend everything was fine in the morning. The last thing she wanted was for him to be uncomfortable.

The clock went off at the usual time, and Dylan slapped it with a muttered groan. He crawled out of bed, every part of his body protesting the effort, and gazed blearily around. But it wasn't his apartment, piled high with blueprints and building plans, it was the spare bedroom in Kate's carriage house.

If only he'd gotten more than five minutes of sleep the night before. But sleep had been impossible.

He was married.

Not a real marriage, but a marriage on paper. And then he'd gone and kissed Kate and practically made love to her. No wonder he'd tossed and turned for hours, trying to decide if she'd actually kissed him back, or if she'd been so shocked and disappointed in his behavior she hadn't known how to react. Maybe she'd even been afraid of him. His stomach lurched at the thought. He wouldn't hurt Kate; that would violate every law of decency he believed in.

"Dammit," he muttered after another glance at the clock. He was due on one of his company's job sites in less than an hour. His men knew he'd planned to get married over the weekend, so they'd roast him if he turned up late after his so-called wedding night.

Dressing quickly, he stepped out of the bedroom, expecting Kate to be asleep.

"Good morning," a cheerful voice sang out.

Dylan stopped cold.

Kate was in the kitchen, barefoot and clad in a skimpy silk nightshirt that reached no lower than her mid thighs and drifted distractingly around her body.

"How'd you sleep?" she asked, not seeming to notice his silence. "I hope the mattress is okay in there. I'll get another one if you'd be more comfortable."

"I slept...fine," he lied. She looked sleepily at ease, and the contrast between her sad face of the evening before and her mood now was astonishing. "You?"

"Great." Kate wiped a smear of jam from her fingers. Apparently she'd been making a stack of peanut butter toast. "Want some?" she asked, holding out the plate.

He silently took a slice and bit down. The hearty bread was crisply toasted the way he liked it and topped with his favorite apricot jam. Without saying anything else she handed him a large mug of coffee, brewed black and strong, then sat at the table, yawning delicately. He didn't know what he'd expected after what happened in her bedroom, but quiet comfort was *not* one of the possibilities he'd imagined.

"I wasn't sure if you took a lunch to work, but I put one together in case you wanted it," she said after a few minutes, waving toward his battered cooler. He'd moved his belongings from his apartment and into the carriage house on Saturday to keep up the appearance of them having a normal marriage.

"You didn't have to do that."

Kate put a hand to her mouth and yawned again. "No big deal."

"Well, thanks."

Dylan let out a breath, his tension draining away. Kate had a big heart. She must have forgiven him for the way he'd acted. And whatever had upset her in the first place, she seemed to have worked it out of her system. As for the lunch, it was probably some of the fussy food stuff that women liked, but he could always order pizza.

Several hours later, when Dylan's stomach rumbled, he eyed the cooler and wondered if there was any point in exploring the contents. It was heavy, but it probably contained bottles of that yuppie sparkling water Kate liked so much. He made a face, then shrugged. The pizza joint that he usually called guaranteed delivery in fifteen minutes.

"Hey, lunchtime, boss," called one of the men. "Time to see what the little lady made for ya. Gotta eat it, you know, or their feelings get hurt."

Damnation. Dylan wished he hadn't said anything about Kate making him lunch, but it had helped deflect some of their more annoying jokes about his brief honeymoon.

His men stood around, watching expectantly as he

opened the battered plastic cooler. His eyebrows shot upward as he pulled out a hearty hoagie roll thickly loaded with roast beef, ham and Swiss cheese. There were two more of the sandwiches inside, along with cookies and chips and barrel-sized pickles.

His foreman whistled.

"Lordy, lordy, it took my wife two years to stop making me finger sandwiches and carrot curls with little toothpicks in 'em. How'd you get so lucky?"

Dylan grunted something unintelligible and took a bite. It was awful nice of Kate to go to so much trouble. She didn't eat much meat, but she'd made sure he had the food he liked.

Maybe the next year wouldn't be so bad. He'd just have to keep things cool and calm. As long as he kept his hands off Kate, everything would work out fine.

Chapter Five

"Hi, guys," cried one of Dylan's sisters from the front porch.

"That's Miranda, isn't it?" Kate asked him in a whisper. Two of his sisters looked so much alike it was still hard for her to tell one from the other, particularly at a distance.

"Yup. She's the interior designer."

"Right." Miranda consulted with Dylan on some of his construction projects.

Kate waved back at her new sister-in-law, feeling strangely nervous about coming face-to-face with the O'Rourkes again. Everything had been so rushed getting ready for the wedding, she hadn't had time to think about anything else. Now she felt responsible for Dylan being in a position he hated…lying to his family.

Miranda called inside the house. "Heads up, everyone, the newlyweds are here."

Within a few seconds various O'Rourkes poured from Pegeen's front door, hugging and kissing and dragging them both inside the house. In her own family, she and Dylan would have been politely announced by the butler and her mother would have lifted her cheek for a cool kiss.

She preferred the O'Rourke way.

"Happy one-week anniversary," Beth said, radiant as she nursed her new baby.

"That's right. Surprised you're here, bro," commented Kane, giving his wife and infant daughter a tender glance. "Thought you'd be having a candlelight dinner, or something else appropriate."

Dylan froze.

Oh, dear. Kate winced. He had that glazed, deer-caught-in-the-headlights expression on his face. *She'd* remembered their one-week anniversary, but hadn't dared bring it up; the happy little milestones that meant so much to most new brides were off-limits to her.

She smiled at her new family and snuggled close to her husband. It was like snuggling up to a brick wall, so she poked a surreptitious finger in his side. "We're celebrating tonight. Dylan has a surprise planned, but he won't tell me about it, will you, darling?"

"No," he said flatly.

She poked him again, hoping he'd smile or do something to prevent his family from wondering if something was wrong. "I have a surprise planned, too," she said. "But I don't think he's guessed what it is."

Dylan gritted his teeth. Obviously there were pitfalls to marrying Kate that he hadn't considered. Like anniversaries. It had never occurred to him that newlyweds celebrated one-week anniversaries. Of course, according to his family he was notoriously unsentimental.

"You haven't guessed, *have* you, Dylan?" Kate prodded.

He looked down into her anxious eyes. She was counting on him; they'd never get away with their plan unless everyone believed it.

He tapped her nose with the tip of his finger. "Does your surprise have anything to do with that bag from a lingerie store you brought home yesterday?" He'd intended the question to be light and teasing, instead it came out low and intimate.

For an instant she looked startled, then a faint blush spread across her cheeks. "I didn't think you…saw it."

"I saw. And I can't wait for my surprise."

The flags in her cheeks grew brighter and she ducked her head against his shirt, just like a shy little girl. She was warm and soft and smelled so nice he wanted to bury his face in her gold hair.

"You're about to discover one of the joys of being married," Patrick said, dragging Dylan's attention back to reality. "I love Maddie's trips to the lingerie store."

"Lately it's just been for maternity wear," Maddie added, patting her swollen tummy. "I have a twisted husband. He still thinks I'm sexy."

"You are," he insisted, seeming astonished she'd think otherwise.

Sexy?

Dylan thought Patrick was nuts. There was nothing wrong with the way a pregnant woman looked, but they were hardly swimsuit models. It even seemed sacrilegious to think a pregnant lady was sexy. Then a vision of how Kate would look if she were pregnant went through his head and he changed his mind. She'd be beautiful.

No.

With an effort he forced the vision away.

"Such serious thoughts," Kate teased. He was probably the only one in the room who could see the worry lurking deep in her green eyes. "Promise you won't tell anyone about your surprise for *me*. I refuse to be the last one to know."

She'd cleverly given him an out, just in case the family tried to pry the secret of his nonexistent anniversary surprise from him, and he smiled appreciatively.

"I promise. They won't get a word from me."

"That's good." Kate put an arm around his neck and drew him down to a kiss. Their lips clung for an endless moment before she drew away. "I…umm, I should…help. With dinner," she murmured.

Dylan wanted to drag her back, and he cursed his lack of control. *He* should have ended the kiss, not Kate.

Apparently they were the last to arrive, and everyone drifted to the kitchen, discussing the past week and arguing amicably about the Seattle Mariner's chances of going to the World Series. That is, Dylan, his brothers and Beth argued the point, Kate and his sisters weren't interested in baseball, though Kate had cheerfully attended live games with him in the past.

Every few minutes she flitted to his side, saying something teasing or affectionate and snuggling up to him in the most distracting way. Hell, how was he supposed to keep his distance when she was acting like a normal bride with satin sheets and candlelight on her mind?

Especially when she kept putting it into *his* mind.

With an effort, he focused on the moment when she'd gotten embarrassed and put her face on his chest. It had reminded him of when she was little, with all those sweet, shy butterfly ways that had captivated his younger self.

"How does this taste?" Kate asked, appearing in front of him again.

"What?"

"This." She popped a cucumber slice coated with salad dressing into his mouth and waited anxiously.

It was a tasty herbal dressing and tasted fine, though he wasn't a big salad eater. "That's good. Did you make it?"

"Yes." Without warning Kate threw her arms around his neck and plastered herself against him. He tasted the same tangy herbal flavor in her kiss, and as much as he wanted to push her away, his body wouldn't cooperate.

The gold silk of her hair caught on his fingers as he cupped the back of her head, and the edges of his self-restraint eroded at the imprint of round breasts and slim hips.

"Hey, you can celebrate your anniversary later," said a nearby voice. An instant later something icy dropped between the back of his neck and collar.

"Brat," he yelped, jumping backward and glaring at his sister.

"What happened?" Kate asked.

"Shannon put ice down my back," Dylan said, squirming as he tried to retrieve the offending cube.

"I'll get it."

As Kate pulled his shirt from his jeans he concentrated on Shannon, instead of the way his wife's fingers spread across his skin, warming it.

His wife?

A sensation colder than ice went through his chest.

Kate wasn't his wife, not in the real sense of the word. The only reason he'd thought of her that way was because of how she'd just kissed him, and that was only for show. Girls like Katrina Douglas didn't marry guys like him, not for real.

"I'll do that part," he muttered when Kate began tucking his shirt back into his jeans. The damage she could do to his control was more than he wanted to risk.

When Kate flitted off again he drew a breath of relief. The week had been so busy he hadn't been able to do anything about his plans for enlarging the carriage house, but he'd start tonight. Once he could shower and get through the evenings without falling over her, it would be easier.

"So, why *did* you come to Sunday dinner?" Kane asked quietly, startling him. "Naturally we're thrilled to see you, but even if a one-week anniversary celebration seems silly to you, it probably means something to Kate. When you get married, your wife comes first."

Dylan's jaw tightened. He was grown now and didn't need lectures from his big brother. "Kate *does* come first."

"You got married a week ago, you didn't go on a honeymoon, and you're at the family dinner instead of spending one of your first free days together. That doesn't sound like you're putting her first."

Kane was in his all-knowing-big-brother mode, an impulse no doubt strengthened by his recent entry into fatherhood. Dylan could confess the truth of his marriage, he even *wanted* to reveal the truth, but he'd kept his own counsel for so long it was impossible to change.

"We'll celebrate tonight, but Katydid is anxious to get

to know the family better," he said. "It means a lot to her, becoming an O'Rourke. You know what her folks are like—I've met marble statues warmer than the Douglases."

"You can say that again. I just don't want to see you two having trouble."

"It's a little early for that. We just got married."

His brother gave him a speculative look, and Dylan met his gaze with a stolid one of his own. The only trouble he had with Kate was his nagging awareness of her. Their friendship would return to normal once the year was up and everything could go back to the way it used to be.

He wanted normal.

He wanted the days when she'd stop at the office and try to convince him to attend one of her blessed charity events and he could be as stubborn as he liked, only giving in occasionally so he could see her smile. Or when he'd show up with baseball tickets, and she'd go along with him to eat garlic fries. They'd never done anything special, just comfortable friendly stuff.

"I hope so," Kane murmured. "It's a wonder Katrina didn't give up years ago and just marry someone else, so don't screw things up now."

Dylan frowned, wondering exactly what his brother meant, but when he started to ask, Pegeen sang out, "Dinner's ready."

At the large dining room table they sat with bowed heads as Pegeen said grace. Kate's small hand rested in his, and for some reason Dylan's chest ached at the feel of it.

He wanted her to be part of his life, but he'd never liked change, especially after his father's death. And they were in the middle of something that could change them forever.

* * *

Kate sat in the truck, half drowsing as Dylan drove back into Seattle. At this time of the year it wouldn't be dark until nearly ten, and the long rays of evening light were gold on the trees.

After a week of Dylan acting quiet and withdrawn it had been a relief to have an excuse to touch him. She'd sort of gotten carried away with the kisses and hugs, but she needed to touch him the way a bird needed to fly.

"I got pastrami and roast beef for your lunches this week," she murmured sleepily. "Unless you want something other than sandwiches."

"No, they're great. Much better than I usually eat."

"Is Swiss cheese okay? I can get cheddar tomorrow if you'd prefer."

"Swiss is my favorite. But that reminds me, I have new checks and a credit card for you to start using."

"You have what?" Kate sat upright, grabbing the shoulder strap of the seatbelt for leverage.

"I set up a checking account for you and ordered a credit card in your name."

"Dylan, I have my own checking account. And credit card."

She'd had her own credit card since she was thirteen. For a while she'd spent money like it was candy, trying to get her parents' attention. It didn't work. The accountant simply imposed a monthly limit—far greater than any teenager should ever have—on her account.

"For the next year you're going to use mine."

She glowered. It was bad enough he was insisting on doing the remodeling of the carriage house out of his own pocket, but she wasn't going to spend his money for everyday expenses.

"No, Dylan, I'm not."

"Don't argue with me, Katydid."

"Why not? You're being completely unreasonable."

He pulled through the electric gates in the back of the mansion grounds and slammed to a stop. "You're the one who wanted this thing to look real."

Since this *thing* was her marriage and the dream of her life, she didn't take kindly to him putting it that way. "Spending your money won't make one bit of difference."

"Maybe, but I'm not going to look like a man who can't support his wife."

Kate rolled her eyes. "Nobody's going to say that. Besides, it's not like we're really married." She made a helpless gesture with her hand, both frustrated and amused. Dylan was so old-fashioned in his thinking, with a code of honor carved in stone. His pride was dead set on showing he wasn't a fortune hunter, that he wasn't going to get a single material advantage from their so-called marriage.

"I may not have the kind of money your family does, but I'm not broke, Katydid. The business is doing great, and I have a number of successful investments. Unless you're planning on cleaning out Tiffany's once a week, we're okay."

"I'm not big into jewelry, you know that."

Still frustrated, Kate slid from the high seat of the truck and started up the winding road toward the carriage house. Though it was in the middle of the city, the mansion and carriage house were surrounded by old forest growth. She liked the peace and privacy, but she'd live in a broken-down shack if Dylan was there.

A muffled curse came from behind her, then the throaty hum of the motor.

"Get in the truck, Kate," Dylan ordered, sticking his head out of the window.

"I feel like taking a walk." It was a lie. Her strappy sandals were terrible for walking, but she stepped to the side of the road so he could pass. Unfortunately her feet sank into the forest loam, so she wobbled and nearly fell.

"Dammit, Katydid, get back in here before you break an ankle. This is a lousy way to get out of an argument."

"It's a stupid argument."

"No, it's not."

Kate stopped and put her hands on her hips. "I know you're archaic in your thinking, Dylan, but in the modern world, people actually form partnerships when they get married, with women contributing to expenses."

"Not when a guy like me marries a girl like you."

"Huh." Kate stumbled as she climbed back onto the road. Dylan wasn't going to haul her into the truck like a caveman, so she hunched her shoulders and headed for the house. He could just creep along behind her.

"*Hell.*"

Dylan threw on the brake and strode after Kate. He didn't know why he was so determined to pay for their household expenses, but it seemed important. The world probably thought he'd fallen into a plushy situation getting married to the heir of the Douglas mansion and the only child of Isabelle and Chad Douglas. He had to know, in his heart, that he wasn't getting anything out of it.

It was ironic. In all the years he'd known Kate he'd never once thought of marrying her, and now everyone probably thought he was the worst sort of opportunist.

"Kate, wait."

She kept walking, turning the last curve in front of the carriage house.

"Katydid, please don't be like this."

Dylan took her by the shoulders and turned her around. His breath went out in a rush at the confused pain in her eyes. What did she want? If only she'd tell him, then maybe he could do something about it.

He brushed a hand over her hair and sighed. She was so lovely, so young and untouched. He didn't *want* Kate to know how nasty the world could be, but things could get ugly fast. As much as he hated admitting it, he might not be around to protect her.

"Baby, maybe it's just pride, but I don't want anyone thinking I married you because of the money."

"Nobody that matters thinks that."

"Maybe. Maybe not. But let me do this, because it matters to me."

Kate opened her mouth, then closed it again, her gaze locked with his.

"For goodness's sake. Are the newlyweds having their first dispute?"

The voice and question, so much out of the blue, shocked them both. In a single smooth movement Dylan spun around, putting himself between Kate and the man standing by the house.

"Who are you?" he asked bluntly. "And why are you trespassing on private land?"

"I'm—"

"It's Richard Carter," Kate said, evading his protective arm. "One of Grandmamma's lawyers."

"I'm not trespassing, I entered using the electronic gate control my client gave me before her death," Carter murmured, his shrewd gaze moving back and forth between them. "I just thought I'd come by and see how things are going. Your grandmother was very concerned for your happiness, Miss Douglas."

"She's Mrs. O'Rourke now," Dylan snapped, enraged.

How could anyone stand there and pretend Jane Douglas had given two hoots for her granddaughter's happiness? The old witch had only cared about the family name and reputation, and now she was trying to run Kate's life from the grave.

All at once he was glad he was helping Kate.

Nobody had the right to manipulate someone else's life. There was nothing wrong with having money, but the Douglases were a bunch of spoiled rich people who'd never learned to do a decent day's work or worry about anything except their own comfort.

But Kate was different. She cared about everybody. When it came right down to it, Katydid might be spoiled, but she was one of the nicest people he'd ever known.

"Ah, yes," the attorney murmured, a faint light gleaming in his eyes. "As you know, Mrs. O'Rourke, I've been charged with executing your grandmother's will and the attached codicils. Your birthday is coming soon, so I'll need to see the marriage certificate to ensure the conditions have been met."

"All right. Come inside and I'll get it," Kate said, sounding weary.

"No," Dylan said firmly. "Mr. Carter doesn't need to

come in. In fact, I think he can wait until tomorrow to see the certificate, or go look it up for himself. Our marriage is a matter of public record."

"Mr. O'Rourke, I—"

"And you can give Kate the electronic gate key," he interrupted. "She'll decide who has access to the property and who doesn't."

The attorney's eyebrows shot upward. "I should think you'd want to ensure your wife's inheritance is secured."

"My wife's inheritance is of no concern to me," Dylan said harshly. "I'd sooner turn the place into a city park, but if Katydid wants that old mausoleum, she can have it."

"Is that what you were arguing about. The house?"

Dylan knew he was being baited, and he made an attempt to calm down. "Not that it's your business, but we were arguing because I want my wife to use the accounts I've established for her. I'm a productive member of society, Mr. Carter. I intend to support my family. Katydid can use her own money for charity work."

An odd smile crossed the lawyer's mouth. "Most men wouldn't care—"

"I'm not most men."

"No, I can see that. Believe it or not, I do understand your feelings on the matter."

Kate made an exasperated sound. "Nobody's trying to understand *my* feelings."

"I'm trying, sweetheart." Dylan ran the back of his hand down her cheek and along her jaw. "Why don't you collect the gate key from Mr. Carter, then get ready for my surprise."

"Oh." A light blush pinkened her cheeks. "It's our

one-week anniversary," she explained as she took the key control from the attorney. "We have…plans."

Dylan watched as Kate climbed the steps. Her hips swung gently, molded by the sundress she wore. It was a pretty thing, with ties at the shoulders that a little tug would have unfastened quite easily…

With an effort he chased his thoughts in a different direction.

"You and Katrina have been friends for quite a while," Mr. Carter commented.

Dylan tensed, reminding himself that Kate *did* want her family's old mansion—God alone knew why—and that he'd married her so she could keep it.

"We met when she was almost five. My dad was their weekend handyman."

"Hmm, yes. You also worked for the Douglases, at least until you were eighteen," the attorney murmured.

"So you don't think I'm good enough for her, because I used to be on their payroll. Is that it?"

"Only if you married her for the wrong reasons—I'm a working man myself, Mr. O'Rourke," the other man said mildly. "I'm quite fond of Katrina. I only want her to be happy."

"I want the same thing."

After a long, searching look at Dylan's face, Richard Carter nodded. "Yes, I believe you do."

Dylan's feelings were mixed as he escorted the attorney to the front gate. Despite everything, he thought Richard Carter actually *was* fond of Kate. But he was also charged with carrying out the conditions of Jane Douglas's last will and testament. If he suspected the marriage was just for show, who knew what kind of trouble he could make.

"Interfering old bat," he muttered as he strode down the hill to get his truck. Jane Douglas was not his favorite person. In fact, except for Kate, the entire Douglas family was on his blacklist.

The bottom floor of the carriage house had never really been modernized. The expansive area that had once sheltered horse-drawn vehicles had changed little over the years. Even the far corners were dusty, filled with cars the Douglas chauffeurs had once babied before newer automobiles were acquired and moved into the main garage.

There was an early Daimler, a Bentley, even a Rolls Royce Silver Ghost, and Dylan shook his head as he pulled his truck into the space by Kate's battered Volkswagen. It was practically a crime to park that beat-up Beetle next to those old classics. Maybe if it was restored it would be okay, but not looking that way.

He'd have to do something about her car. He wanted Kate driving something that didn't look like it was held together by nothing more than chewing gum and paper clips. In fact…Dylan looked more closely at one of the windshield wipers and saw there actually *was* a paper clip holding it together.

"Oh, for Pete's sake." He scowled and pulled his toolbox from the back of the truck.

"What are you doing?" Kate asked as she came downstairs.

"Fixing this. What mechanic ripped you off, claiming the damn thing was repaired?"

She grinned. "Nobody ripped me off—I fixed it myself.

I was late for a meeting and it was raining, so I just twisted the paper clip around that thingy and it worked fine."

"Why didn't you take it to be repaired later? Jeez, Katydid, you need a keeper."

Kate's smile faded as she contemplated kicking Dylan right in his scrumptious rear end. "It works, and it's perfectly safe."

"That's what they said about the Titanic—right up until she sank."

"My car isn't the Titanic."

"Maybe not, but I'm getting you a new VW. This thing isn't fit to take out on the street."

Her jaw dropped, then she scowled. "I don't want a new car. I like this one."

"Don't tell me it has character. Character can get you killed." Dylan kicked one of the tires and the hubcap fell off. "See what I mean? Whatever sentimental attachment you have to this hunk of junk isn't worth it. You can turn it into a planter if it's that important to you."

"Fine, but I'll buy my own car," she snapped.

He just gave her that stony-faced look he'd perfected all week and didn't say anything else. Drat him. The only time she'd been able to get near Dylan was at his mother's house, and he'd only permitted it then so no one would know the truth about them. And now he was high on his pride and dignity, especially with her grandmother's lawyer coming to check up on the legitimacy of their marriage.

She could just scream.

"Dylan—"

"Forget it, Kate. I told you the way it's going to be."

She glanced around the garage and got an idea.

"Fine, but only if you take one of the cars Grandmamma left me. Take your pick." Her hand waved, encompassing the shadowed interior of the garage.

Dylan rolled his eyes. "Not a chance. Those cars are worth a fortune. Besides, trucks are my speed, you know that."

"Yeah, I know." She grinned mischievously and he gave her a wary look. "So maybe you'd like the one over there."

Kate walked to the far corner and Dylan couldn't help following. Pure curiosity, he told himself. He had to find out what mischief she was planning; it was one of the reasons Katydid still seemed like such a kid to him, she was always up to something.

With a flourish she pulled the tarp away from the prettiest old truck he'd ever seen. Built no later than 1910, it was shiny black beneath a layer of dust and seemed to be in perfect condition.

"No," he said automatically, though a part of him wished he could take the thing apart for the sheer fun of working on something so old.

"If I let you buy me a car, then you have to take this one," she told him.

Dylan twitched the tarp back into place and faced Kate. He could afford to buy an antique truck for himself if that's what he wanted, and he wouldn't accept this one as payment for acting the way a husband was supposed to act. Never mind that he didn't feel like a husband. Their marriage certificate said otherwise.

"Kate, I'm not accepting something so valuable, and that's that."

"Then I'm not accepting another car, either."

She turned on her heel and stalked away.

Dylan rubbed his throbbing temples. Damn, she was stubborn.

And so much for things working out easily. Their arrangement was becoming more complicated than he'd ever expected, starting with the moment he'd said, "I do."

Chapter Six

A couple of weeks later Kate stumbled out of her bedroom, yawning tiredly. It was hard to sleep knowing Dylan was still annoyed with her over the car and the credit card thing.

Huh.

He was mad because she didn't want to spend his money. There was something almost comical about that.

Of course, she supposed a man's pride wasn't anything to laugh at, especially when it was Dylan's pride. He had the most stiff-necked attitude. She should have known he'd get worked up about her family's money, particularly with them living on the Douglas estate, rather than a place he was paying for.

Yawning again, Kate started a pound of bacon frying on the stove. She wanted extra for Dylan's sandwiches that day, to add variety. The amount of protein he ate made her shudder, but she supposed he worked so hard that he burned it all off.

And now he was coming home and working on the carriage house all evening, installing electric doors on the garage and getting building materials delivered for the work on the apartment above.

Double drat.

Her cozy little home was going to get a lot less cozy once he was done.

A little later, as she put Dylan's sandwiches together, Kate heard his bedroom door open. She hastily cracked several eggs into the frying pan and dropped bread in the toaster.

"Breakfast is almost ready," she called.

Dylan came in, fastening his shirt. "You don't have to cook for me. I don't expect it."

He said that every morning and evening, and like every other time, she shrugged. "I don't mind."

His face was grim. "At least you should wear something a little less…that is, something more suitable for cooking."

Perplexed, Kate looked down at her nightshirt. Was there supposed to be suitable clothing for cooking? Her parents' and grandmother's cooks had worn uniforms, but that was silly. "What's wrong with this?" she asked.

"For one thing, there's nothing to protect your skin," Dylan growled. "Your legs are completely bare."

"Not really. See?"

She plucked at the silk nightshirt, pulling it higher. Her legs weren't bare, the shirt went halfway down her thighs. She'd thought about buying something really revealing to tempt Dylan and demonstrate she was quite grown-up, but she hadn't found the time, or the nerve. In the meantime, her nightshirts would have to do. Besides, she wasn't doing anything unusual. She always wandered around in whatever was comfortable.

"For God's sake, don't do that!" Dylan growled.

"Do what?"

She wanted to scream. Why was he such a bear? He snapped at her more and more as the days went by— like the time she'd come down to the garage to say good-night. Instead of saying good-night himself, he'd snarled at her, saying she should get decently dressed before going outside. And that was the most he'd said the whole evening. She'd done everything she could think of to make things easy and comfortable so he wouldn't be inconvenienced by their marriage, but it wasn't enough.

The back of her throat ached. It was the same feeling she always got when the people she loved weren't satisfied with her best, or ignored her, or didn't approve. Maybe it wouldn't be any different with Dylan. Maybe love *wasn't* enough to make everything work out, no matter how much you wanted it to.

The pan on the stove crackled and Kate spun around.

"Oh, no."

The eggs were brown, burned beyond redemption.

She grabbed the frying pan and shoved it in the sink, but the careless action made the grease sizzle and pop onto her wrist. She stifled a cry and pressed the burned spot to her mouth, not wanting Dylan to know. He'd just say I-told-you-so, as if he knew everything and she was still a kid to be scolded.

"You have to put it in cold water," Dylan said gently. He swung the faucet to the other side of the sink and turned it on. "Give me your hand, Katydid."

It was like all the times he'd rushed to her rescue and tears poured down her face. Things would have been easier if they'd stayed children, but they hadn't. Why was it okay for him to grow up, but not her?

"I'm sorry it hurts. I'll call the doctor," he murmured.

"I don't need a doctor."

"You're crying."

Her heart was crying most of all, but she shook her head. "It just startled me. Your lunch is ready. Maybe you could pick up something on the way for breakfast."

"You already have a blister."

"Really, it's okay."

Dylan closed his eyes and kept Kate's wrist under the running faucet. It was all his fault she'd burned herself, picking on her over those skimpy nightshirts. Even now her tight bottom was snuggled into his groin, reminding him of how little she was wearing.

He'd practically exploded when she'd pulled the hem up. Was she wearing anything beneath? He'd stopped her before he could find out, and now his less noble side was kicking him for being…noble.

It's Katydid, his better half reminded.

The child whose sweet, charming ways had gotten him into a heap of trouble when he was a kid himself.

The reminder didn't help.

Thinking about Kate being grown up had never been his favorite subject, but it was hard to ignore with her traipsing around in nightshirts that revealed each womanly curve.

Like now.

He looked down and saw that her nipples had hardened, crowning her breasts and standing out against the thin silk fabric. Every detail was revealed as he leaned over her. Setting his jaw, Dylan forced himself to release Kate and step backward. The promise he'd made to her on their wedding night kept going through his head. There wouldn't be any repeats of that damned kiss.

It was killing him.

"I'll get some ice." He took ice cubes from the freezer, wrapped them in a dishcloth, then hammered them into a flexible pad. "Here."

Kate drew a ragged breath. "You're going to be late," she whispered as he wrapped the cloth around her hand.

"I'm the boss, it's allowed." Yet he was usually on time, and if he didn't get out soon, he'd have more trouble than ever keeping his promise. "But if you're certain you're all right, I'll get going. I want to get back early—we have the hospital fund-raiser tonight, right?"

"Yes, we should leave by six."

It was one of Kate's pet projects, for the children's hospital, and it would be their fifth public appearance as husband and wife including Sunday meals with his family. He wasn't looking forward to it since her snooty friends would be there, as well. On the other hand, the hospital was a good cause, and not every rich person in Seattle was a loss. Some of them were pretty nice.

Like Kate.

Kate was rich. Born rich and spoiled with every material belonging that could be showered on a child. And she still always thought about other people before she thought of herself.

"I'll…uh, see you later," he murmured.

Grabbing the cooler and thermos waiting for him on the kitchen counter, Dylan hurried out the door.

Despite his best intentions, Dylan arrived home late. He called out a hello and jumped into the shower to scrape off the inevitable layers of grime. The company had contracted to remodel several of the old brick-faced buildings in downtown Seattle, and plaster dust was a constant companion.

He was in the living room, struggling with his cuff links, when Kate came out. "Could you help me with these?"

Her nimble fingers made quick work of the links, which was a good thing. After spending the day with sweaty construction workers, Kate smelled so great it was tough keeping his hands to himself.

"By the way, I asked Kane to lend us his company limousine," he said.

"Is something wrong with the truck?"

"No, but I don't like valet parking."

Her forehead creased. "You've never minded before."

"We weren't married before."

She sighed. "I don't care what other people think, and I thought you didn't, either."

Dylan blinked, surprised. "I don't. But you're getting enough flak because I'm your husband, you don't need more because you arrived at a formal occasion in a Dodge Dakota instead of a limo."

"Nobody that counts will think twice about how we arrive." Kate planted her hands on her hips and fixed him with an intent gaze. "I mean it, Dylan."

He opened his mouth, then closed it again, realizing

Kate was serious. She'd never minded going places in his truck, even when his truck used to be a twenty-year-old Chevy he'd rescued from the junkyard. Why would he think she'd changed?

"If that's what you want."

"It's what I want. I'll be ready in a minute."

Kate went into her bedroom and dropped the robe she was wearing, then pulled her dress into place. Made of emerald green velvet, the gown swathed her body like a sarong, baring her shoulders and the upper slopes of her breasts. The gown fitted snugly until it reach her mid thighs, then fell in graceful folds to the floor. It was more risqué than what she normally wore, but being married to Dylan wasn't normal.

"Kate?"

"Coming." She grabbed the miniscule purse matching the dress and hurried into the living room. A strangled sound came from Dylan and she frowned. "Is something wrong?"

"Is that what you're wearing?"

Kate glanced down at the green velvet, then up again. "Well, yes. I picked it up yesterday."

"But that's…are you even *wearing* underwear?"

She plastered a casual smile on her face. It would be nice if he felt possessive, but he was probably just shocked that little Katydid was wearing something so revealing.

"There's only so much you can fit under a dress like this."

He scowled. "Fine. Let's go."

Her skirt was tight enough to cause trouble climbing into the Dakota, and Dylan finally lifted her up with a muffled curse. Her heart beat faster at the sensation of his strong hands on her waist, and she wondered what he'd say if she suggested he slide those hands up her legs, under the velvet, to check for himself if she was wearing anything beneath.

Dylan's mood didn't improve, so when they arrived at the banquet hall, she hesitated about playing the role of a happy new bride. If she pushed too hard she could lose any ground she might have gained.

"I'll get us some drinks," he muttered, disappearing before she could make up her mind.

"It's good to see you, Katrina," said a languid voice the moment she was alone.

Exasperated, Kate turned around. "Hello, Tilly."

The platinum blonde smiled an artificial smile. Honestly. How could Dylan think she was friends with anyone like Tilly Haviland? The woman was an energy sponge, sucking up life from anyone around her.

"My goodness, imagine you having to run out and get married so quickly. No wonder you couldn't invite anyone."

Kate's eyes narrowed. She knew exactly what Tilly was suggesting. "Actually, it was a private family wedding, with only our closest friends. And since I've been in love with Dylan for years, it didn't feel quick to me."

Tilly's jaw dropped. "But darling, he's hardly your type."

"Actually, he's exactly my type. You know—hard-working, honest, reliable...*faithful.*"

It could have been a low blow since Tilly's slouch of a husband was the complete opposite of faithful, but

Tilly played around even more than her husband. They deserved each other.

"I'm so lucky," Kate continued in a blissful tone. "Dylan is the kind of man you can always count on. Of course, I understand if you're a bit envious, he *is* incredibly sexy."

The other woman's lip curled. "Perhaps in a rough sort of way. Personally I prefer more polish in a man."

That was it.

Nobody criticized Dylan, he was the greatest guy in the world, even if he drove her nuts. "Tilly, you're such a—"

"I brought you a drink, darling," Dylan said, sticking a glass in her fingers, then grabbing her elbow as if worried she'd resort to violence.

Tilly gave them a tight smile and drifted away more quickly than normal. Kate gripped the fluted glass filled with champagne and strawberries, fighting the temptation to go after Tilly and dump it down her silicone-enhanced cleavage.

"What was that all about?" Dylan asked.

"Stupidity. I think all that bleach she uses on her hair is frying her brain cells," Kate said.

Dylan grinned. He'd heard Katydid defending him, and the sincerity in her voice had given him a warm, foolish feeling around his heart. "You can't go to war because she thinks you married beneath you."

Kate turned, an astonished look on her face. "You don't understand. Tilly is jealous. She's dissatisfied with her life and wants everyone else to feel that way, too. Most of the time I feel sorry for her."

"But not tonight."

"It's different tonight."

She obviously didn't want to explain, and Dylan wasn't certain he wanted to know why it was different. He was having enough trouble figuring her out these days.

Idly, Kate turned the stem of the champagne glass in her fingers, then took a sip. One of her eyebrows lifted. "This is ginger ale, not champagne."

"I thought you'd prefer something without alcohol."

Her lips pressed together. "You mean I'm not ready for adult beverages. I'll be twenty-seven next week, not seventeen. When are you going to accept that I'm not a kid any longer?"

Dylan shifted uncomfortably, the question striking too close to home. Intellectually he knew Kate wasn't a child, but in his heart she was still that little girl he'd first known, beautiful and elusive and untouched by the horrible things in life.

"You don't like alcohol. Remember?"

"I…oh, never mind."

All at once Kate smiled, put her free arm around his neck and gave him a passionate kiss. It took a moment to collect himself, then he glanced around, wondering who she was trying to impress.

"Who are you looking for?" she murmured.

"Richard Carter or one of his law associates."

"I haven't seen them." She tugged on his collar and he leaned down. But instead of explaining, she kissed him again. This time he relaxed into it, tasting the strawberries from Kate's drink and her sweet essential essence. His blood ran heavy, sinking low into his groin and desire dug claws into his self-control.

Obviously it was the dress.

The thing was designed to drive a man off his rocker.

Kate must have spent a fortune on the gown, which ought to infuriate him since he was certain she hadn't used his credit card or checking account to buy it. Yet all he could think about was discovering if she *really* wasn't wearing underwear or covering her up so he wasn't tempted by so much skin and innocent sensuality…and no other man was, either.

"Mmm." Kate drew back and smiled, the picture of a starry-eyed bride. "Are you okay?" she asked when he didn't respond.

"Yeah." He was okay except for the agony in his groin and the way he still wanted to be kissing her.

It was a problem that worsened as the evening progressed.

They ate from a buffet of expensive finger food, when he would have preferred a decent steak. The only good part about the food was seeing Kate eat strawberries dipped in dark chocolate, then lick her lips with delicate swipes of her tongue.

She also stuck to him like glue, leaning into him, brushing his face with the tips of her fingers, and wiping away tiny smears of lipstick from his mouth whenever they kissed. Which was often. His body churned with sensual whiplash, and he had to keep reminding himself it was all an act. He kept trying to fix in his mind the way she'd looked the day they met, the sweet and shy and charming four-year-old, but the mental picture kept dissolving into an adult Kate, with undeniable adult curves.

"It's too bad Kane and Beth couldn't come," she said after they'd visited with the director of the children's hospital and she'd promised to arrange for a local mime troupe to entertain the kids.

"They're not going anywhere for a while," Dylan murmured. "Beth won't leave the baby, and Kane won't leave Beth."

Kate's smile wavered for some reason, then she kissed the corner of his mouth again. His blood surged with predictable speed. "She's very lucky."

"Jeez, Kate." He took a step backward and she followed in perfect tandem. "Maybe you should be more restrained."

Her green eyes blinked. "But if I'm not affectionate, people will wonder if there's something wrong with our marriage," she said. "At least anyone who really knows me."

She was right.

She was just being Kate, but that was the problem— loving, naturally affectionate Katydid, acting the way she'd always acted with anyone who'd let her. It must have been hell for her growing up in the Douglas family; they were the least demonstrative people he'd ever seen.

Dylan glanced around the large room—feeling more trapped than ever—and saw the last person he wanted to see.

"Damn," he muttered.

Kate turned the same direction and wrinkled her nose as the stately, silver-haired Richard Carter approached them. That's all she needed. He'd asked a number of questions when she'd brought her marriage certificate into the office, watching her with his shrewd eyes. It wasn't an experience she wanted to repeat.

She leaned against Dylan for both warmth and comfort, and his arm slid around her waist. Richard Carter couldn't know about their arrangement. He might suspect the truth, but what could he do? They hadn't broken the law and she had every intention of making her marriage real; she just needed time to convince her husband. *That's* why the lawyer scared her, because he could take away her last chance to be with Dylan.

"Buck up, Katydid. It's going to be all right," Dylan whispered in her ear.

The warmth of his breath made her shiver and she looked up. He was strong and sure and everything she'd ever wanted. She forgot all about Richard Carter and her grandmother's will with its unpleasant codicil.

"Have I ever mentioned how great you look?" she asked.

"You mean I clean up okay in a tux."

Kate smoothed the lapel of his tuxedo. "I mean you're a great looking guy. Your brothers can't hold a candle to you, in a tux or anything else. But you're particularly sexy in jeans."

"Hah." He grinned down at her. "You must be blind. I'm the ordinary O'Rourke. Remember?"

"There is nothing ordinary about you," she said. "Why do you think Tilly Haviland is so jealous of me? She knows she'll never have anything a hundredth as good."

A chuckle rumbled through his chest. "I thought you were going to scratch her eyes out earlier."

"Not quite that bad." She shrugged. "But dumping strawberries down that silicone cleavage would have been satisfying."

"Silicone?" His eyebrows shot upward.

"You don't actually think her bustline is real, do you?"

Another shiver went through her as Dylan traced her collarbone, his gaze drifting lower to her own more modest cleavage. "I wouldn't know, I was too busy catching my breath over your dress, sweetheart. I keep wondering what keeps it…up."

Kate swallowed, her breasts tightening. She remembered how it felt to be touched there, Dylan's fingers and mouth flooding her with heat and anticipation. Yet even as she remembered, she thought about what he'd just called her.

Sweetheart?

The only time Dylan called her sweetheart was when he was playing his role as an adoring fiancé turned husband.

Disappointment filled her at the same moment she heard Richard Carter discreetly clear his throat. "Mr. and Mrs. O'Rourke, how nice to see you."

"Mr. Carter, I didn't realize you were a patron of the children's hospital," she said politely.

"I have a variety of interests."

Yeah, and one of those interests was nosing into her marriage. Kate was tempted to point out that her grandmother's will had only said she was to live with her husband on the Douglas estate for a year—*sex* wasn't specified. Grandmother would never have been that vulgar. Boy, Nanna Jane must have been a real fun date. She'd probably considered the marriage bed to be a necessary, but unpleasant, duty.

Still, the conditions in the will were an excuse to be affectionate with Dylan. It was the first time Kate had been able to touch him so freely, and she planned to take advantage of every opportunity.

The three of them chatted for a few minutes, then Dylan's arm tightened around her waist. "I'm sorry to rush off, sir, but I'm anxious to get Kate home. She had an accident in the kitchen this morning and should get some rest."

Mr. Carter looked concerned. "Nothing serious, I hope."

"No," Kate said quickly, then tipped her head up at her husband. "Really, I'm fine, Dylan."

"Then we'll just…rest."

His suggestive tone was unmistakable and heat instantly rose in her face. If only she could believe he was sincere and that the sensual promise in his voice and eyes was real.

But it wasn't, and she knew she'd be spending the night alone.

Again.

Much later Dylan lay in bed, his body so primed he couldn't sleep. He'd never been this way before. If there was a woman he couldn't have, either because of circumstance or her own choice, then it was fine.

So why was he going crazy over Kate?

Maybe it was that forbidden fruit thing. They were living in cramped quarters and he'd promised not to kiss her again. Unfortunately she wasn't held to the same promise. Her act as a loving bride was damned convincing…at least it was convincing his body.

Stop, he ordered. Katydid was a sweetheart, but she wasn't permanent.

He raised his arm and tucked it beneath his head, staring at the ceiling. When he'd originally built the carriage house apartment, Kate had asked him to leave as much of the original structure intact as possible. Because of that, natural wood beams ran through the ceilings, and richly colored braided rugs were scattered across hardwood floors more than a century old.

At least he'd convinced her to enlarge the windows, styling them after the old ones.

God, Dylan thought, the *hours* he'd spent on those windows, finding matching antique glass, working forever to get them just right. But it had been worth it when Kate smiled and flung her arms around him.

"Stop," he growled to the silent room.

He was blowing it.

Kate was a friend, not a lover. She'd asked him for help because she trusted him. Her defense of him to the Haviland woman had rung with sincerity and given him a great ego boost, but he couldn't read too much into it.

Dylan turned over in the bed for the hundredth time. Kate was in bed as well, less than thirty feet away. She'd taken off that expensive, seductive dress and was wearing one of those expensive, seductive nightshirts. Nightshirts that shouldn't be seductive at all, but on her, they were.

He groaned and punched his pillow a couple of times.

His response to Kate's public kisses was difficult to ignore, no matter how he tried to keep cool in private. Maybe he should spend an occasional night on the couch at the office, to calm things down. Besides, the way things were going it was the only way he'd ever get some sleep.

Right.

He had a plan.

Monday afternoon he'd call and say he couldn't make it home. Clean and simple. With any luck he could just leave a message on the answering machine and not have to explain. Explaining would be hard, especially since he didn't want Kate to get worried or uncomfortable about him living with her and he wasn't certain he could lie to her.

In the meantime he'd just have to remember his cuddly bride was putting on an act worthy of the greatest actress ever born…even though his body was too dumb to know it.

Chapter Seven

On Monday Kate typed away on her computer, lost in her tale about an intrepid girl called Little Stuff. Little Stuff had shown up in previous stories and was so popular Kate's editor had asked for a new series with her as the lead character.

The story was rolling along, so when the telephone began ringing Kate decided to let the machine pick it up…then heard Dylan's voice.

"Kate, it's me. You're probably not in…"

She ran for the phone.

"…but I needed to let you know I won't be home tonight."

Kate snatched up the receiver and was stunned to hear a dial tone. He hadn't even said goodbye, or see you in the morning, or explained *why* he was spending the night someplace else.

A sick feeling hit her tummy, and she sank onto a chair. Was it another woman?

Surely not.

Dylan knew it had to appear they were happily married. He wouldn't just casually go out with another woman when he thought so much was at stake. Would he?

Her heart instantly denied the possibility, but her head kept chewing on the question. Dylan was a man who had needs, *physical* needs. Of course, they'd only been married for a few weeks, so it wasn't as if he'd been deprived of sex for ages. She'd gone her entire life without sex, so she knew it was possible, if not comfortable.

Talking to someone else would help.

Kate tried to think of who she could confide in and was more depressed than ever. The social circle she'd grown up in didn't lend itself to close friendships, and most of her college friends had moved away in search of bigger and better jobs. As for her parents, they'd have heart failure if she tried to discuss something more important than the weather.

Dylan was her best friend.

He wasn't good at opening up to her, but he'd always been there when she needed someone. Over the years she'd talked to him, laughed with him, and cried on his shoulder, which didn't leave many options when it was Dylan she needed to talk about.

With an effort Kate dragged herself back to the computer, her story no longer the least bit interesting. Little Stuff might be able to solve any problem, but Little Stuff's creator was swimming in the dark.

* * *

When Kate heard Dylan put his key in the door the next evening, a feeling of both relief and despair swept over her. At least he wasn't spending *two* nights away, but that didn't explain why he'd stayed away in the first place.

Well, she wouldn't ask.

If she started acting like a jealous shrew he'd never want to stay married.

Yet a recurring thought nagged at her…did she want to stay married with things like this? Even if Dylan decided to make their marriage real, could she spend the rest of her life in a limbo where the man she loved was as close as the sun's warmth and more distant than the stars?

Ice condensed in Kate's stomach and she bent over the sink, washing her salad makings and trying not to cry. Trying not to think about the years of wishing and hoping and wanting.

"Hey, Kate," Dylan called.

She swallowed, plastered a noncommittal expression on her face, and turned around. "Hi."

"Looks like you're fixing dinner."

"Yeah." She'd taken care to dress in slacks and a blouse, nothing he could call inappropriate for cooking, though she hadn't been sure he would be back for dinner or anything else.

"If you've fixed enough, I'm hungry." He gave her an inscrutable look that reminded her they weren't really married and didn't answer to each other. She didn't have any business asking where he'd been, because they were just roommates with a complicated legal situation.

"No problem, I'll just put on a steak. Dinner will be ready in a few minutes."

"Great, I'll go wash up."

Kate pulled a steak from the refrigerator and sea-soned it with garlic and cracked pepper, the way Dylan liked. She'd fixed fettuccine Alfredo and broccoli, but it was easy enough to add a steak for Dylan. It was a vain hope that he'd eat much of the broccoli and salad, though maybe if she kept putting vegetables on the table he'd eventually add something healthier to his diet.

In the bathroom Dylan wadded up his soiled work shirt and threw it against the wall, bothered beyond be-lief that Kate hadn't said a single word about him being gone the night before.

Didn't she care?

She was a woman. Women were naturally curious. She should have asked why he'd called like that and where he'd been. She should have said something that would have made him feel self-righteous and smug about his decision to cool things down by staying out all night. It wasn't as if he'd enjoyed sleeping on the office couch.

"I'm a damned jackass," he muttered as he got in the shower.

It wasn't Kate's fault he was having trouble keeping things calm. She'd tried to be helpful. No matter how often he said she didn't need to cook for him, she got up early every day and made breakfast and a packed lunch. She fixed dinner, except when they attended a social function, and didn't ask anything else of him except that in public they appear to be normal, loving newlyweds.

Hell, she wouldn't even use his money, something that was making him nuts. And he really didn't see why it was such a big deal. The money wouldn't be more than what he'd have spent on his own apartment, so it was like paying rent. He paid his dues and didn't take anything from anyone. He'd even repaid Kane's loan for starting his construction business at twice the usual interest rate. Of course, Kane had been upset about it, but that was too bad.

A man stood on his own two feet.

He'd accepted the responsibility of marrying Kate for a year so she could get her inheritance, and it was a pleasure to thwart Jane Douglas's attempt to put a stranglehold on her granddaughter's future.

Pleasure?

Right.

Dylan twisted the shower faucet and let cold water stream over him. He missed the way things used to be with Kate—the comfortable teasing, the occasional charity event, the nights he brought over a pizza and a movie for the VCR. She'd given him an electronic key to the gate when he converted the carriage house and insisted he keep it afterward. He'd liked that, liked knowing she trusted him and that she counted on him when she was in trouble.

But why hadn't she asked where he'd spent the night?

Why wasn't she pouting and upset?

Maybe she'd ask when they were eating dinner. Yes, that's when she'd start pushing for an answer.

Dylan pulled on his clothes and walked out, rubbing his hair dry with a towel, strangely cheered by the conviction that sooner or later Kate would start asking nosy questions.

"Smells good," he said, watching as she pulled out a perfectly seared steak from the broiler.

She flashed him a casual smile and forked the meat onto his plate. "Take that while I get the salad."

A creamy pasta dish sat on the table, along with the inevitable vegetable bowl. Kate never tried to make him eat anything he didn't want, though she always made enough for two. Maybe he'd eat some salad tonight to make her happy.

"How did you…sleep?" he asked once they were seated.

"Fine."

The calm, composed way she said it irritated Dylan all over again. He'd given her an opening, a chance to ask him about *his* night, and all she'd said was *fine*.

"I almost forgot," Kate murmured after a long moment. "Your mother called." She got up, fetched a piece of paper, then sat down again and served a small portion of pasta, vegetables and salad onto her own plate.

A phone message?

That was it?

"Er…when did she call?"

"About nine." She twirled a long swirl of noodles around her fork and ate it with evident pleasure. "It's a good thing we're not going anywhere together for a couple days. I loaded the sauce with fresh garlic, so you won't want me kissing you for a while."

Since Kate's kisses had never been anything but sweet, Dylan couldn't imagine a little garlic would change them. That was the problem. Even after a cold shower he was getting worked up, watching her lick Alfredo sauce from silverware. Obviously her appetite hadn't been affected by curiosity, or by his absence.

"My bid was accepted on the Hansmeir building complex," he said finally.

She smiled. "That's terrific."

"We're going to be awfully busy on it for the next year, at the very least. You didn't…?" he hesitated.

"Didn't what?"

"I know J. R. Hansmeir is acquainted with your father. You didn't say anything to your father about my bid, did you? That is, nothing that might have influenced J.R.'s decision?"

Kate stuck her fork into a piece of broccoli. Here she was, trying not to fall apart, and Dylan was asking if she'd used her influence with someone her father barely knew.

"No, I didn't. Did you want me to?"

"Of course not," Dylan said harshly. "I just wanted to be sure *you* hadn't. It's important to me to win contracts without any undue influence because of you or my family."

Technically she *was* family, because technically she was his wife. But apparently that didn't figure into his thinking. "I wouldn't do that without talking to you first," she asked. "Don't you know that?"

"Uh…yeah."

She blinked rapidly and swallowed the last bite of her salad. More than anything she wanted Dylan to kiss her and sweep her away to the bedroom, but not because she'd blackmailed him into it with tears. It wasn't just wanting sex, it was the idea of being held—the kind of holding that sank into the center of your being and made the rest of the world go away.

At least she thought it would be that way.

Sometimes she thought she needed Dylan more than she needed to breathe.

"You don't have anything to worry about," she said carefully. "Mr. Hansmeir might know my father, but they aren't friends. My father is the kind of dilettante that irritates real working men."

"You don't think much of him, do you?"

"Mr. Hansmeir?"

"No, your dad."

Kate shrugged, losing what little appetite she'd had. "I don't really know him, except that he likes to travel and buy expensive art. It's not as if we've ever sat down and talked."

Dylan was silent for so long she was convinced she'd shocked him, but her poor relationship with her parents shouldn't be a surprise. He'd watched her grow up, and he knew they'd been too busy with their travels and social life for a child. In some ways Dylan's father had been a better parent to her than Chad Douglas. She still remembered Keenan O'Rourke's warm, wise eyes that seemed to see more than most people and his strong, capable hands that could fix anything.

"Don't misunderstand," she murmured. "I love my parents, but we're not close."

She'd give anything to be more important in her mother and father's lives. But it wasn't likely to happen. They certainly hadn't rushed home to meet her husband, or do anything except make her feel vaguely guilty for not arranging her wedding at a more convenient time for them.

"I know," Dylan said finally. "Well, anyway. I'm going to get more measurements on the new rooms."

He left without asking if he could help with the dishes, though he usually did, and Kate sat for a long while at the table, her heart aching.

If the entire upper floor of the carriage house was remodeled it would make a spacious home, ideal for a growing family. The original conversion had used the center space, which had originally belonged to her great-great-grandfather's head groom. She wouldn't care if Dylan was knocking out walls for their children, but he was knocking out walls so he wouldn't have to be close to her.

That hurt so much she could hardly bear it.

And she didn't know how to change his mind. The plan that had seemed so clear and possible a few weeks ago now seemed like the height of folly. She wanted Dylan, but she also wanted her friend back—the friend that would never have spent the night away from their home, leaving her to wonder what he was doing. But the worst part was, she now had to wonder if *that* Dylan had ever existed at all.

The old servant's quarters were warm and dusty, and Dylan scowled as he wrote down precise figures. He didn't need the measurements. He'd already planned and figured the additions and knew exactly what had to be done.

But he also needed to get away from the way Kate tugged at his heart. No one could ever call Katydid a "poor little rich girl." She was too alive and full of fun, but she was alone in a way he didn't like to think about. No wonder she'd turned to her parents' employees when she was in trouble—she certainly couldn't turn to *them*.

But if he and Katydid were such great pals, why hadn't she asked him about last night?

It was a question that gnawed at him over the next two days. Kate kept busy on her computer, at the same time making arrangements for a wine and cheese tasting party to raise funds for a child care center. She seemed to be involved in everything from soup kitchens to the historical society, and he discovered there were serious people listening to her when it came to raising money and managing resources.

By Thursday afternoon his head was splitting and his foul temper had alienated three of his crew chiefs.

"Can I get you anything?" asked his secretary with a nervous expression on her face.

He drew a breath, trying to keep from offending yet another undeserving person. "No, Janice. I'm fine."

But he wasn't fine, and his hand hovered over the phone. Maybe he should call Kate and tell her he was sleeping at the office again. Yet his hand dropped and he stared dully at the calendar. Something was bothering him, as if he'd forgotten something important.

All at once he groaned and jumped out of his chair. *Kate's birthday.*

Dylan rushed out to his truck, fishing his keys from his pocket. He'd never forgotten Kate's birthday; not even when he was seven and could only afford a candy bar and wildflowers as a gift.

His week was going from bad to worse.

Kate leaned down and painted her toenails a pale shade of pink, then stuck her foot out and wiggled it. She usually didn't give herself a pedicure, but she felt like pampering herself. It was her birthday and she'd gotten into the habit of making the day special for herself.

Sighing, she leaned back on her elbows and thought

about Dylan. He was still in such a lousy mood, she was considering using his credit cards, just to make him happy.

Jeez, weren't men supposed to complain about their wives spending too much money?

"Kate?" Dylan called from the living room.

Her eyes widened. Dylan didn't usually come home from work until almost six…when he did come home. Her mind instantly shied away from thinking about the night he'd spent somewhere else.

"What are you doing home so early?"

"I thought we'd go out to dinner." The door opened and a hand appeared, holding a bunch of pink tulips. "Happy birthday, Katydid."

A slow smile lifted the corners of her mouth. She loved tulips, they were such happy flowers. "Come in, Dylan."

He stuck his head inside. "I have reservations on the waterfront at your favorite restaurant."

"Aren't you tired? We could wait till Saturday."

"I'm going to work on the remodeling this weekend."

"Oh." If it had been any other excuse Kate would have been happier, but the remodeling was a sore point for her. "Okay, but I don't mind fixing something."

"Come on, let's go out. You shouldn't have to cook on your birthday, and it'll be nice going somewhere we don't have to put on a big newlywed act."

More of Kate's pleasure faded. She might not be the sexiest woman in Seattle, but it shouldn't be such a burden for him to be affectionate. "That'll be…nice."

"Do you need the shower, or should I go ahead?" he asked.

"You go."

Dylan had the damnedest feeling he'd done some-thing else wrong, but he didn't know what it might be. Still, he cleaned up in record time and hurried out to find Kate already dressed. She looked too perfect for a guy like him, and it boggled his mind that she was actually his wife. On paper, at least. He missed the way it used to be when they were just friends—when she was Ka-tydid, and he was the boy she could talk into anything.

God, she didn't even look like Kate; she was Katrina Douglas, elegant and sophisticated in a designer gown, and his irritation welled up again. Irritation that she didn't seem to care where he'd spent Monday night. It was childish and illogical and he tried to ignore it.

"Ready?" she asked.

"Sure."

The evening went well until he pulled a jewelry box from his pocket and handed it to Kate. "Happy birthday."

Her face went still at the sight of the emerald and dia-mond drop earrings inside. "They're lovely."

"They go with your green dress from last Friday."

"I thought you didn't like that dress."

He shifted uncomfortably, because it was the woman inside the gown that had bothered him so much. "It's a little low cut, that's all."

"And?"

"And nothing."

Her fingers snapped the velvet box shut, and she turned it around a couple of times, unreadable thoughts racing across her face. "What's going on, Dylan? Five thousand dollar earrings for a friend's birthday? It's be-cause I won't use your dumb checking account and credit card, isn't it?"

"They're not dumb."

Kate got up, shoved the earrings at Dylan and walked out of the restaurant and down to the waterfront. The cool breeze off Puget Sound didn't soothe the turmoil in her heart or the pain that Dylan had caused by using her birthday gift as a way of paying off his idea of a debt.

Things were so much more complicated than she'd thought they'd be, with Dylan's pride and everything else complicating her simple plan to make him fall in love with her.

An evening ferry chugged in the distance, seagulls reeling and screaming above it. The distinctive scent of the ocean mixed with evergreens and city life—so familiar in Seattle—filled her senses. She closed her eyes and tried to find peace.

"Please get in, Kate."

From the corner of her eye she saw Dylan had brought his truck around from the parking lot, and she sighed. Getting into a snit wasn't the way to his heart, but there didn't seem to be any other way to get there, either.

They were both silent as he negotiated the traffic back to the Douglas estate. Dylan was more remote than ever, and she didn't know whether to swallow her own pride or to stand her ground and make him see reason about the money. It wasn't that she needed to pay her way, but she'd gotten him to marry her under false pretenses and her conscience bothered her, especially when he kept trying to pay for everything.

They pulled into the converted garage and Kate waited for Dylan to get the door for her like always, but he just sat with his hands on the wheel.

"Dylan?"

"I'm sorry I've been so bad tempered the past couple days."

The past few days?

Kate kept her mouth shut…much as she wanted to say something about the past couple of weeks. She knew marriage was hard, but usually there were benefits that went along with the bad, like cuddling at night and knowing that your husband loved you.

"Uh, that's okay," she said finally.

"No. It's just…" He seemed to be struggling with what he wanted to say, then let out a breath and looked at her. "I want to know why you didn't ask a single question about me being gone on Monday. Don't you want to know where I was?"

Lord.

It was all she could do to keep from screaming at him. Of course she wanted to know. She was dying inside every time she thought about who he might have been with, and why, and how much *she* meant to him. Or if there was a *she* in the first place.

But she couldn't say anything like that because Dylan would immediately realize how she felt.

She undid her seatbelt and slid out of the truck.

"Where are you going, Kate?"

"Obviously nowhere."

She sensed Dylan's irritation in the way he slammed the truck door and stomped after her, but it bought her time to find an answer to an impossible question.

Chapter Eight

"Kate?"

Kate unlocked the door at the top of the stairs, knowing Dylan was close on her heels. She pushed inside and dropped her purse on the couch.

As birthdays went, this one really stunk. But she had to pretend Dylan's question wasn't a big deal...even though it was putting a stake through her heart.

The door slammed shut.

"Why, Kate? Why didn't you ask?"

Men. They wanted it both ways. If you were jealous, then you were being unreasonable and catlike; if you *weren't* jealous, you were unreasonable and didn't care enough. Both were equally upsetting to a man and his ego.

"It isn't as if you're really my husband," she said, attempting to stay calm. "I'd appreciate it if you don't advertise an affair because of the legal situation, but we each have our own lives." Yet even as Kate said the word *affair*, her heart was breaking.

"*What?*"

"I'm just asking you to be discreet."

Dylan didn't know whether he was flabbergasted or just plain angry. No, he was *furious*. Angry wasn't strong enough to describe the way he felt. No matter how it had come about, Kate was his wife.

His wife.

And there weren't going to be any affairs, for either of them.

"Sorry, but I don't live in the world of bored wealthy marriages and casual affairs," he snarled. "As long as we're married I won't be sleeping with anyone else and neither will you. We'll just have to control any urges we might have until after the divorce."

"Urges?" Kate repeated thoughtfully.

Before he was tempted to offer to satisfy any of Kate's urges, Dylan stomped back down to the carriage house garage. But even there he couldn't stand still, and he went outside and plunged onto the walking trail that meandered around the hill. The Douglases had maintained a slice of Cascade mountain wilderness in the heart of the city—not because they were dedicated to the environment, but from a snobby determination to set themselves apart from everyday people.

"Damn. Damn. *Damn.*"

His curses echoed through the growing darkness. After two circuits around the perimeter of the estate he wasn't calmer. Almost against his will he veered into the back gardens of the mansion and stared up at the hulk-

ing building. Maybe if the old place had ever been filled
with love and laughter, it might not seem so grim and
lifeless. It might even have been an interesting example
of period architecture, but all he saw were the seeds of
unhappiness.

Kate's unhappiness.

Dragging air into his suddenly tight lungs, Dylan
leaned against the trunk of a spreading maple tree.

There were so many times Kate had been hurt by her
parents' neglect or her grandmother's criticism. She was
an essentially happy person, but the shadows in her soul
were reflected in the work she did, helping others. In
some deep, unspoken place she understood other people's pain and wanted to heal it.

The sound of someone moving in the garden came
from nearby, and he wasn't surprised to see Kate emerge
from the shadows.

He might understand her better than ever before, but
he was still angry. With good reason, he might add. The
things she'd suggested appalled him. He crossed his
arms over his chest and waited.

"Hi," she said softly.

Hi? That was all? Apparently she didn't feel any more
communicative than she'd been earlier in the week.

"What are you doing here?" he asked. "It isn't safe
to be out alone."

"Yeah, who knows who I might run into on a private estate, with sophisticated electronic security protecting it."

"You could trip and fall in the dark."

"So could you."

He could counter that by saying he was a man and a

construction worker accustomed to keeping his balance in tricky spots, but he knew better.

"Did you really think I was having an affair?" The question exploded out of him, and he winced.

Starting the argument over again wouldn't change anything, and he'd already ruined Kate's birthday— though he didn't see how a pair of emerald earrings could be such a big mistake.

"I didn't…I don't know."

Kate rubbed her arms, and he saw she didn't have a sweater. The evening had grown cold, a weather front moving over the city like a gray ghost. It didn't matter to him with his tough hide, but she got cold on a seventy-degree day.

"You should have brought a wrap if you were taking a walk."

"I'm not a child," she said automatically.

"I didn't say you were a child, I just said you need to wear something warm."

"Like I wasn't capable of being responsible for myself or accepting the consequences. Look, I just thought we should talk. I don't like fighting with you, Dylan."

He didn't like it either, and he was horrified by his lack of control…and by his primitive possessiveness.

But how could she believe he was the kind of man to sleep around? She'd known him most of her life. Depended on him. He'd agreed to help her, why would he mess everything up with an affair?

"I wouldn't have married you if I was involved with someone," he said at last. "I said I'd help."

"You weren't thrilled about it."

She had him there.

"Nobody has the right to control someone else's life," Dylan said. "That's what your grandmother tried to do, and it was wrong. I just didn't realize…"

"What?" Kate took a step closer. The faint fragrance of her perfume drifted around him and his blood surged with heat. "You didn't realize what, Dylan?"

No way was he going to confess the unruly responses of his body. And how could he explain the rest of it? He knew Kate was only his wife on paper, but that wasn't the way it felt. His father had raised him with a strict code of behavior. A wife was a wife, and a man supported his wife, took care of his family, and did right no matter how tough it might be.

"Never mind, Katydid. I'm sorry I spoiled your birthday dinner. I know I've been difficult lately, but the money stuff makes me uncomfortable."

In the faint light escaping from the clouded sky above, he could see her chewing on her lip. "If it's really that important, I'll use the checking account for the household expenses," Kate said. "But not for my clothes, and I won't let you buy me a car."

"Your car is a hunk of junk."

"So I'll buy one for myself."

No.

For a moment Dylan worried he'd shouted it aloud, then realized it was only in his head. Kate was turning out to be more stubborn than he'd ever realized, which bothered him, because it was something else he'd missed seeing about her.

"Please, Kate, if you want a Beetle, let me buy you a new one. The new model is just as spiffy as the original. They're great. I might even like having one myself."

A giggle rose in Kate's throat, and she clapped a hand over her mouth.

Dylan wasn't the spiffy type, he was a rugged truck sort of man. With his looks he could even pose for one of those truck commercials where a gorgeous guy rolls up in a cloud of dust, gets out and leans casually against the fender. He wouldn't even have to say a word. Women would fall all over themselves buying trucks, and men would buy them, too, because he was their sort of man.

"So if you insist, I'll keep the Beetle after our divorce," Dylan said, sounding as if it was perfectly reasonable.

This time Kate couldn't keep from chuckling.

"What?" he demanded.

"*You* behind the wheel of a compact car?" Her laughter rang out and she saw a glint of white in the shadows as Dylan grinned.

"Are you saying I'm oversized?"

"I think you're the perfect size…to drive a truck."

"Ever the diplomat. Come here, Katydid." The shadows shifted, and she sensed his arms were outstretched.

With a mixture of sorrow and relief Kate walked into the hug. It was just like when they were kids, and he was trying to make her feel better because of something that had happened. Comfort and sympathy, not love.

But he was warm and big and hard, and she leaned against him, accepting the comfort.

"Sorry about the earrings," he murmured, his breath stirring the hair on her temples. "Maybe I *was* trying to pay you back. Sometimes my pride is worse than a tiger on my back. I just can't stand to have anyone think we're together because I'm after your money."

"We're not together."

"Nobody knows that."

She'd hoped he'd contradict her, but it was a vain hope.

Dylan slowly eased them both to the ground and settled her against his chest. He crossed her arms over her stomach and put his arms over hers, surrounding her with warmth. City noises were filtered out by the woods and night air, with only the looming Douglas mansion reminding her that the rest of humanity wasn't far away.

The house was dark and silent, not much different than when her grandmother had lived there. Kate had a vision for the house, restored and filled with light, a center for community activities and a showcase of Seattle history. The historical society could run it as a nonprofit foundation, and she'd serve on the advisory board.

"Dylan," she said slowly. "The people who really matter don't think anything about us being married. They see a highly successful businessman who doesn't need anyone's money. You're honest and fair and trustworthy. There might be a few people with dirty minds and unhappy lives who want to believe the worst of everyone else, but their opinions shouldn't count. Not ever."

He stayed silent for a long while, then sighed. "You're right. And it's really about me. I grew up a certain way, with certain beliefs, and taking care of a wife is one of them. Instead I'm living on a palatial property rent free, you're spending your own money on expenses, and it's like I'm being…kept."

"That's ridiculous. You aren't being kept. You won't take any money for the remodeling and all the other work you've done, and that costs loads more than a few steaks."

"Yeah, but the remodeling was my idea."

True.

But she had her own demons to deal with, including a conscience that twinged more each day. At least Dylan was talking to her again and not being so stone-faced and impossible. Her spirits lifted. Arguments sometimes cleared the air. Maybe things would be different now.

In the meantime she wanted to enjoy being held by the man she loved, though his embrace was that of a friend, not a lover. Besides, she wasn't the tiniest bit cold with the length of Dylan's body down her back. She just wished she had more experience telling if a man was aroused—then all at once she realized she *could* tell and her spirits went higher than a helium balloon on a hot day.

"Tell me something, Dylan," she murmured. "Did you ever think…uh…about dating me, back when we were teenagers?"

"Did I what?"

The question had obviously surprised him, and his tension became palpable.

Darn.

"You know, when we were just kids." Kate deliberately made her voice casual, as if it couldn't possibly matter now and she was only asking out of idle curiosity.

"You're *still* a kid."

She rolled her eyes, though he couldn't possibly see it. "You're only two years older than me."

"Two and a *half* years." He said, making it sound like centuries separated their birth dates.

Brother. She was in love with the most obstinate man alive. "Kane is eleven years older than Beth, and he manages to see her as a woman."

Dylan shifted minutely, trying to ease the agony in his lower abdomen. He must have been crazy to sit down and put Kate between his outstretched legs—either that or his subconscious was working double time against him. She made him feel as eager and charged as a teenage boy still trying to score his first kiss.

Why the sudden curiosity about something she ought to understand? Poor boys might date rich girls in books and movies, but they didn't do it in the world he lived in.

"So, did it ever cross your mind?" Kate asked again. "I mean, about asking me out?"

"No," he said bluntly.

"Oh."

Her sigh was so soft he barely heard it.

"Jeez, Kate, what difference does it make now?"

"None. But we were friends, and I didn't look that horrible, did I?"

"Well, no, but we were a million miles apart back then. Still are, for that matter."

"A million miles? That's not how it feels to me," she muttered, so low he barely heard it. In fact, he wasn't certain he was *supposed* to hear it. Though considering how agonizing it was to have her snug bottom pressed into the inseam of his slacks, she had a point.

He swallowed a groan.

Talking about the past wasn't going to solve anything, but he knew Kate wouldn't let it go at a simple answer. Women were bulldogs when it came to certain things, and she wasn't an exception.

"Katydid, nothing can change the fact that my dad was just another one of your parents' servants when we met—the weekend handyman. And I'm like my father,

I want to work with my hands. My brothers chose professional careers, but I'm a woodworker. Dad wanted to make furniture; I build buildings."

"What's wrong with that?"

"Nothing. But there's miles of difference between a rich society family and a guy who gets sweaty making a living. And I'm not interested in changing—I'll take a pair of worn-out jeans over a tuxedo any day."

Kate jerked away and twisted to look him. "Nobody's asking you to change."

"I was just trying to explain why dating you never crossed my mind. Hell, can you imagine how your father would have reacted if the kid who used to mow his lawns tried to take his only daughter out to dinner? He would have had me arrested."

"*My* father? You have to be kidding—he wouldn't have noticed."

"Maybe, but your grandmother would have had me shot. There wasn't a chance in hell she'd risk having her precious bloodline sullied by someone so far beneath her."

"You aren't beneath anything."

"Tell that to your grandmother!"

"I would, but she's not available." Kate's voice was choked all at once and Dylan winced. She'd loved Jane Douglas, though it was never certain the same affection was returned.

"I'm sorry, Katydid. I shouldn't have said that."

Kate rose, evading his hand. She carefully brushed small bits of leaves and dirt from her dress, and he recalled how pretty and happy she'd looked at the restaurant before he'd given her the earrings. Some hero he'd turned out to be, using her birthday gift as a way to salvage his pride.

Cripes, *that's* why the earrings were such a big mistake. They'd been about him, not her.

"I've always been proud of who you were," she said quietly. It was so dark he couldn't be certain, but it looked like tears had streaked down her face. "I never wanted you to change. You're the one who thought something was wrong with one of us, and I'm beginning to wonder if it was me who didn't measure up to your standards."

"No! That isn't what I—"

With a swirl of shadow and sweet fragrance she disappeared, moving so quietly he wasn't certain which direction she'd gone.

"Kate?"

Nothing but the evening breeze answered him, and Dylan hit the back of his head on the broad tree trunk. Something was happening he didn't understand, and it was moving so fast the ground was getting ripped from beneath his feet.

I've always been proud of who you were...

Kate's words filled an empty place in his soul, a place he hadn't known was empty. It was like when she'd defended him at the hospital fund-raiser. Passionate, unshakable approval. Their differences didn't seem to matter to her.

"No." He forced the denial through gritted teeth, because he didn't need anyone's approval. He was doing what he loved, even if it wasn't what his mother and father had originally hoped for their family when they'd left Ireland.

The faint patter of raindrops sounded around him, but he was reluctant to move. He'd never wanted to hurt

Kate or make her believe he didn't think well of her. She was so special, filled with love and generosity and laughter, while he was just an ordinary guy. Sooner or later she'd realize it, and that's when he'd lose her.

Some things can't be lost, son. Kate sees you with a woman's heart.

Dylan's spine went rigid as the timber of his father's voice rang true and clear in his ears. But it couldn't be. He was only imagining it because he knew how fond Keenan had been of the lonely little girl who'd followed them around as they worked.

Right?

No answer came except the suggestion of a rich chuckle that rustled through the leaves above him.

Chapter Nine

Kate drew a brush through her hair, thinking so hard she didn't even see her reflection in the dressing table mirror. Instead she focused on the tulips Dylan had given her the night before.

Birthday tulips.

Dylan had gotten up and left before dawn, but he'd written a note saying he would be back for dinner. A lot of things had been said last night, and she'd revealed more than she had intended; if he took the words apart he would know she loved him. But there was nothing new to that, he could have figured it out at any time.

Sighing, Kate laid the brush on the table and went to her computer. She'd never missed a deadline with her editor, and she didn't intend to start now. Yet it was hard to focus on the story and it took her longer than normal to write Little Stuff's adventures.

Twelve hours later Kate had succeeded in focusing so well that she didn't hear Dylan arrive home until he called out her name.

"Katydid?" he called again, tapping on her door. "Are you busy?"

Kate hastily pulled up an Internet page, concealing the work she was doing. "No. Come in."

She glanced up and saw that Dylan's jeans were caked with mud below the knee. A rag was wrapped around his upper arm and bloodstains adorned his ripped shirt sleeve.

"What happened?"

Dylan swung a hard hat along his leg. "What do you mean?"

"Your arm, that's what I mean," Kate said, exasperated. "There's blood all over it."

He shrugged. "Took some skin off with a nail, that's all."

The idea of Dylan getting hurt made her stomach tighten, but he'd think she was silly if she made a fuss. "You probably want to take a shower, but then I should put on a clean bandage."

"Thanks." He glanced around the room, then looked back at her desk. "You seem to spend a lot of time on the computer."

"Just surfing the Internet," she said, waving her hand dismissively. Part of her wanted to tell him about her books and the prestigious children's literature award she'd just been nominated for, but she wanted him to love her for who she was, not what she'd accomplished.

It was so mixed up in her head.

Did he really believe that she was too immature and

shallow to value hard work and talent over the sort of wealthy anachronism her family had become?

"The Net?" He sounded puzzled.

"It's useful for research on…stuff."

"Oh."

A guy like Dylan probably wouldn't be caught dead surfing the Internet. Kate only used the Net for quick fact-finding and e-mail, but he didn't need to know that.

"I'm sorry I lost track of the time," she said hastily. "I'll get dinner together, then I have to go to a board meeting for the children's hospital."

"I thought the regular board meeting was last week."

"Some property near the hospital just went up for sale," Kate explained as she rushed around the kitchen. "We're going to discuss acquiring the land for the new orthopedic clinic."

Dylan frowned and unbuttoned his shirt. He didn't like the thought of Kate going out alone at night in her ancient car; if she'd only be reasonable and let him buy her a new one then he wouldn't have to worry so much. "You're talking about the old Candler property."

"Yes."

"I heard it was for sale. I'll drive you to the meeting."

"You will not." Kate shook her head and pointed to his arm. "You're going to take a shower. I'm going to fix that cut with a sterile bandage. Then you're going to have a relaxing evening at home."

"Kate—"

Her face set stubbornly. No matter how he reasoned with her while she tended his scratched skin, she refused his company. As a result he was left in the silent apartment, fuming as she backed her car out of the garage.

He had to admit the motor purred like a kitten, but he'd rather have her safe in the truck.

More than that, he'd rather have her safe at *home*.

It was a shock to realize he resented the meeting that took Kate away from him. The children's hospital was an important community service, and he didn't have any business minding one way or the other, but he did.

"Dammit, *no*."

Feeling trapped by something he couldn't understand, Dylan rigged up lights in the space he was remodeling and tore into one of the walls. The strenuous effort helped him focus, but it didn't prevent him from listening for Kate's return.

He had to get a grip.

She didn't belong to him, and she never would. It would be insane to hang too much on her declarations from the previous night. Katydid didn't lie, but she was a creature of silk and spun gold who didn't belong in his world of sandpaper and steel rebar. A man and woman who were that different might manage to be friends, but they'd never survive a lifetime of marriage.

It was time to put up more barriers, and this time he would keep them up.

Several hours later Kate walked through the opening Dylan had cut between the living room and the space beyond.

"Hey, Dylan."

"Hey." He didn't look up, and she shifted her feet.

"It's stuffy in here. I'll set up the fan."

"No," he said sharply. "It'll just move the dust around."

Her eyebrows shot upward. She was tired. The board meeting had lasted forever, with various factions disagreeing on what they should do and how much debt the hospital could risk. And now Dylan was uptight again. But everything else faded away when she saw that the white bandage above his elbow was stained with fresh blood.

"Your arm is bleeding again. Let me put on a new bandage."

"I don't need to be mothered, and the real world doesn't stop working because of a little scratch."

His tone sounded so cool she actually shivered.

"It's more than a scratch." The sight of his torn skin had made her sick to her stomach, though she'd tried not to fuss too much about it.

"No, it's not. Go to bed, Kate. I'm too busy to talk." He lifted a hammer and began pounding on the old wall.

She swallowed. Maybe it was just discomfort from his arm and being tired from a long week.

"D-Dylan? What's wrong?"

Dylan looked up, and she saw pain in his dark eyes. "Please, Kate. I can't take any more tonight."

Nodding, unsure of exactly what he meant but certain she couldn't take any more, either, she fled to her bedroom.

Little changed over the next week, except Dylan seemed less angry. Kate found his silent reserve a small improvement, but it crushed her hopes that he'd become more open to her.

Honestly, she fumed. The strong, silent type might be appealing on the silver screen, but in real life living with him was hard. And lonely.

Efforts to persuade the hospital board to purchase the Candler property was taking a significant portion of her days and evenings, so Kate worked late each night on her novel to stay on schedule. Whenever Dylan asked about what she was doing she said something about the Internet, but he kept frowning at the answer.

Early Saturday evening she returned from another interminable session with the board and dropped onto the couch with a weary sigh.

"Bad meeting?" Dylan asked.

She glanced over at the French doors he'd installed in place of an open cut in the wall, and her pulse kicked up.

"Bad enough." Climbing quickly to her feet and shedding her suit jacket, she gave him a smile. "Sorry I'm late. Have you eaten?"

"No. I figured you'd be tired, so I ordered pizza. I'll stick it in the oven to heat."

Tears pricked at her eyes. "Thank you."

It was ridiculous, but Dylan's stomach swooped at the appreciation in Kate's face.

She was such a puzzle. All that time on the computer couldn't be idle Web surfing. There had to be more to it, and she put long hours into her community work. It was much easier to resist her appeal when he thought she was a spoiled princess who just dabbled in charity work.

Resisting?

Hellfire.

Dylan shook his head and wondered who he was trying to kid. Kate had been getting to him even before that kiss on their wedding day. She bothered him. She took a *breath* and it bothered him, and heaven knew her sweet curves were driving him crazy.

"What's going on with the hospital board?" he asked as he slid the pizza onto a round pan.

"Mr. Wayland is unhappy because the property has a condemned building on it," Kate said, brushing past him to the refrigerator.

His nerves tied themselves into a knot at the brief contact, and he nodded, resigned.

That bothered him too.

"There aren't many empty lots in the city," he said after clearing his throat. "And none near the hospital."

"I know." Kate took a thirsty swallow of milk. "It's ridiculous. He says taking down the old building will cost more than we can afford. I say we can't afford *not* to build the clinic. You can't tell kids with broken bones that it was just too much trouble getting them a decent treatment center."

Dylan thought for a moment. "You're right. Tell Wayland that O'Rourke Construction will do the demolition as a donation to the hospital."

Kate lit up with a smile so bright it nearly blinded him. "You will?" She threw her arms around his neck. "Oh, Dylan, you're wonderful."

"Kate…"

Whatever he'd intended to say was lost when she kissed him. It was warm and passionate and filled with her dazzling energy. The world shifted and crackled around them, burning in a fire that didn't consume. It just got hotter.

Of their own accord his fingers cupped her bottom, pulling her tighter against him, thrusting her breasts into his chest. The kiss deepened, turned slow and more intense, and his mind was swept away like a boulder in a flash flood.

But when he twisted and lifted her onto the counter, something in Kate's soft gasps brought a thread of sanity back to him.

"I have to stop," he muttered.

She pulled at the back of his shirt and slipped her hands beneath, kneading the muscles in his lower back.

Once again his thoughts skidded off, obedient to the will of his body. Her fingers slipped inside the waistband of his jeans, and he groaned.

Kate hesitated, unsure if she was doing the right thing.

Was it too soon?

Probably.

Or maybe not.

Drat.

She had to decide before it was too late, but it was hard to know if her heart or head or more primitive instincts were in charge. Dylan's lips nibbled their way down her jaw and she dropped her head back, inviting him to kiss his way down her throat. More than anything she wanted his mouth over her breasts, the way he'd caressed her on their wedding night.

"I'm sorry," Dylan gasped all at once, even as his thumbs traced circles around her nipples.

"For what?" Kate blinked away tears of frustration.

"I promised I wouldn't kiss you again."

"But I was the one who kissed you."

"Oh. Right."

His eyes were darker than she'd ever seen them, so intense, and his gaze dropped to his hands, now cupping her breasts. A quiver of anticipation went through Kate.

She wiggled and realized her legs were wrapped around his thighs, the hem of her skirt pushed up to her hips. Something hard and insistent pressed against her feminine center. There was no doubt about Dylan's response.

She couldn't turn back now.

The room shifted as Dylan put his hands under her bottom again and lifted her. With a small yelp she clasped his neck and tightened her legs around his hips. The movement as he walked intensified the ache low in her stomach, and she shuddered. The wall and ceiling spun as Dylan put one knee on her bed and lowered them both. In the same smooth action he put a hand on her breast, and his mouth over hers.

Oh...*my.*

It seemed impossible to get a breath into her lungs, and she was afraid to move, anyway, for fear it would distract Dylan. Time slowed, measured only by the pounding of her heart and the long slow kisses, so deep there didn't seem to be any beginning or end.

That's Dylan, she thought giddily.

Thoughtful, deliberate, a builder of things.

Through the ringing in her ears Kate thought she heard two dull thuds, and guessed it was his boots landing on the carpet. Her own shoes were long gone, and even as the realization came, he eased down her body, smoothing away the rest of her clothing and rolling down her panties and stockings.

Nibbling kisses followed his fingers, brushing over her knees and calves, spots she would never have guessed to be erogenous zones. But when he rubbed the arch of her foot along his jaw, all heck broke loose in her body. The rasp of his evening beard shadow against her sensitive skin sent heated prickles streaking through her veins.

"I should stop," Dylan muttered so harshly she barely understood him.

Should stop?

Before he'd said he *had* to stop, so maybe he wasn't sure, and Kate had every intention of adding to his doubt on the matter. With a boldness she hadn't known she possessed, she put her arms above her head and slowly stretched.

Dylan stared at Kate in the soft light from the bedside table, his thoughts more scattered than light in a kaleidoscope. He'd pulled her long hair from its conservative knot on her head; it was rumpled, falling sexily around her shoulders, with streamers of gold and platinum scattered across the pillows.

She didn't look the least like the Katydid of his childhood. She was a grown woman with sleek silken lines and rounded curves in all the right places. The little girl who'd followed him around with worshipful eyes was really gone, no matter how hard he'd tried not to accept it, and an unutterable sorrow clawed at his throat.

How long before he lost…

The questions scattered as Kate smiled a dreamy smile and wiggled her toes ever so slightly against his face. Her breasts were drawn tight, still aroused by his touch, and as though drawn to a magnet he rocked forward on one knee so he could trace their sweet curves.

Kate's body was beautifully balanced to her petite height.

Enough for a handful, he thought as he cupped her in his palms. That's all a man really needed. Just a handful of sweetness to drive him mad. He'd just hold her for a minute, then stop. Yet his thumbs moved of their own accord, rubbing over Kate's nipples, making her breath catch again and again.

"Come down here," she whispered, pulling on his shoulders.

His head still warred with his body, but his head was losing. *Fast.*

"Only for a minute."

"Okay. A minute," Kate agreed. She didn't know how much longer she could wait for the deeper joining she craved, and she could only pray his minute would turn into a whole night.

Dylan kissed the very tip of her breast, then drew her deeply into his mouth, shaping her throbbing nipple with his teeth and tongue, while his hand rolled the other between his fingers.

Mmm.

His hands were big and hard from years of long work, and she loved the feel of them.

Kate stared at the ceiling for a dreamy moment. Dylan really did build beautiful things. Even when he was a boy it had been obvious—his love for creating something good and strong, and his gift for making it happen. He built houses people could turn into homes. He built skyscrapers and churches and bridges. Best of all, he'd make beautiful babies.

And of course she was in the middle of her cycle, and her hormones were simply screaming about babies.

She wanted him.

All of him.

Yet it was still a shock when Dylan eased her thighs apart and slid between, and she felt him gently probing her.

Her breath caught as it stung for a moment, and it

took longer than she'd expected to adjust to the age-old rhythm. She'd thought of being with Dylan so often she ought to be good at it, but the discomfort lingered, distracting her from the heat and need beneath.

"Relax, baby," Dylan said, his voice sounding harsh.

He reached between their joined bodies and touched her, dragging a low cry from her throat.

The tension built again.

"That's it." He whispered his encouragement and murmured other dark, intimate things that should have been shocking, yet somehow just made her more excited…more *his*.

Dylan caught the back of her knees and lifted them high. The new angle seemed to please him, and Kate's eyes widened as he thrust even deeper, sinking to the center of her being.

"Let go," he muttered, sounding stressed. "Please, honey, let *go*."

Kate sensed he was holding off, waiting for something, and she knew it was her release.

Briefly she considered pretending, then sensation exploded in her abdomen, taking control, erasing any need for pretense. She cried out and clung to Dylan, losing herself, knowing he was the only one who could keep her from scattering across the universe in countless particles of fire.

Dylan yawned.

Something was different.

Really different.

He woke slowly at the best of times, and he'd spent the night in a deep, dreamless sleep he hated to disturb.

He couldn't remember the last time he'd slept so soundly, then decided that wasn't true. He did remember—he hadn't slept soundly since Kate had made her absurd proposal about them getting married.

Kate?

He lifted his head and looked down at the vision of pink and gold sleeping at his side.

It *was* Kate.

His head hit the pillow again and he groaned. After everything, after all his best intentions, he'd made love to her, and it had been the hottest sex of his life.

Memories of the previous night tumbled through his head, the tastes and sounds and sight of Kate's silky body. She made such eager little noises when he was inside of her, though she'd seemed uncomfortable at first.

Uncomfortable? Dylan frowned, sorting through the befuddled state of his brain, then his stomach did a cartwheel.

Of course it was uncomfortable. Kate had been a virgin.

Sweat broke out on his forehead, and he eased his arm from under her head. Not only had his marriage been consummated, he'd hurt Kate by not being as gentle as she deserved.

And why had it happened? Because she was grateful he'd offered to tear down an old building. He'd gotten carried away and couldn't even blame her damned nightshirts because she'd been wearing a skirt and blouse.

As for the divorce…now it would be a divorce in truth.

Dylan stumbled out of Kate's bedroom, nausea churning his stomach. He needed to think, and the best way he knew how to do that was by getting to work.

* * *

When Kate woke alone she thought the previous night had been nothing more than a pulse-pounding dream, then she crawled out of bed and felt sore in a very feminine location.

A warm, silly smile crossed her mouth, then faded as she wondered what Dylan's reaction would be. She somehow doubted he'd suddenly seen the light and wanted to be a real husband.

A tremor of fear went through her. It had happened too soon. She'd hoped living together would make him see her as sexy and capable instead of helpless and childlike, but there was a proper time to everything. Now he'd feel more trapped than before and would push further away from her.

She took a shower and dressed in a skirt and light summer sweater, trying to decide how to handle the next few hours.

Act normally?

It was probably best, though she didn't feel at all normal. Shaking her head, Kate went into the living room and heard faint sounds from the far end of the carriage house. It sounded like wood being sawed, so Dylan must have decided to spend his Saturday morning working on the new rooms.

An hour later she had fresh blueberry muffins baked, bacon and ham keeping warm on the back griddle, and a fluffy mound of scrambled eggs seasoned and ready to go. Coffee was hot in the pot and the table set.

Sucking up her courage, Kate went in search of Dylan.

"Good morning," she called.

Dylan froze.

"Breakfast is ready."

He turned around reluctantly, wishing there was a time machine that could undo the past twelve hours. He searched Kate's face, and though something unknown lurked in her green eyes, she didn't seem any different.

"Kate, about…last night. It was your…" Dylan stopped, feeling like a babbling idiot. How could he be embarrassed to point out that Kate had been a virgin? "The thing is, I couldn't help noticing it…uh…was your first…time."

"Oh, well, it's every woman's first time once."

"But you were a virgin. I shouldn't have… That is, it shouldn't have—"

"Don't worry about it, Dylan." She shrugged. "It was quite pleasant, and if you'd like to do it again, I'd like that, as well. But let's eat breakfast before the eggs dry out."

Pleasant?

Dylan stared at Kate's disappearing back with disbelief.

It was *quite pleasant?*

What in hell did she mean by that? He might not have been at his best, but she'd gone off like a firecracker, he'd bet his life on it.

He was furious with Kate and even more furious with himself. She was his wife now, no dancing around the truth. They had a legal piece of paper, had made vows in front of friends and family and a judge, and he'd slept with her. So much for his promise to keep his hands to himself.

He'd married Kate so she wouldn't have to sleep

with someone just to get her grandmother's house, and now she acted like it wasn't a big deal that *they'd* slept together.

Women were impossible.

Chapter Ten

Several days later Dylan was still chewing on his frustration, and Kate wasn't helping in the slightest. She gave him enigmatic smiles, acted as if nothing had happened, and was generally turning him into a basket case.

Weren't women the ones who wanted to analyze everything to death?

They'd made love. It had been her first time. But she didn't talk about it or assume their relationship had changed. All she'd said was that it was quite nice, and she was willing to do it again. When she was little Kate used to spill out her heart to him, and now all he saw was a polite mask. It bothered him more than he could understand.

"Do we have any functions or anything this weekend?" he asked Thursday as they ate dinner.

"No."

His knife grated on the plate as he hacked at his succulent stuffed pork chop. He looked at Kate and wondered if she was paler than normal or if it was just his imagination. "Then we can spend Sunday with my family, right?"

"I guess you haven't noticed that I don't commit to anything on Sundays," Kate said, trying to keep an edge from her voice. Making love had complicated things horribly, and it was all she could do to keep from crying over dreams that were breaking apart.

My family. Was that Dylan's way of reminding her that the O'Rourkes weren't her relations? Or was it just her imagination working overtime?

"Yeah, I know. I just…what's wrong, Kate?"

She gathered herself and pinned a smile on her face. "Nothing. Everything is going great with the hospital board now. Our bid has been accepted on the Candler property, and we're just waiting for the environmental study."

"That's good. I'll work with the board on the best time to do the demolition."

"Thanks, but it won't be necessary," she murmured. "I called a bunch of places before you offered, including O'Rourke Enterprises, and Kane contacted the board yesterday. He's going to cover the cost of demolition, so you're off the hook."

Dylan's eyes narrowed. "What if I don't want to be off the hook?"

"You only offered because we're married…sort of married," she qualified. "It doesn't seem fair."

"Dammit."

Startled, she watched him throw his wadded-up napkin across the room. "What?"

"I'll make my own decisions, thank you," Dylan snapped, infuriated. "Tell the board I'm taking down the building, and Kane can redesignate his contribution."

Kate remained silent, staring at him, and he tried to calm down. They had to get back to their old camaraderie, the comfortable teasing and warmth they'd shared before getting married. Kate was special to him, and no matter how frustrated he might be for a lot of different reasons, she was still his friend.

His pride was more hurt than anything.

Quite pleasant.

With an effort he pushed the thought away. Kate was an innocent, she probably didn't know how a comment like that would grate on a man's ego.

He felt guilty, that was the problem. His code of behavior was having trouble processing the fact that he'd made love to his best friend, and she'd turned out to be a virgin.

"Kate, honestly, I want to help the hospital out," he said more quietly. "And it isn't just because of you—though I have to point out you never used to be shy about asking for donations from me before."

"Oh." She blushed, the way she used to when he teased her, and something tight in his chest eased a little.

"Come on, admit it," he continued in a light tone. "You were always after me to donate to some cause or another. And you kept dragging me around to your fundraisers whenever possible, so nothing much has changed. I know how to say no, if that's what you're worried about."

She laughed. "Okay, okay. I'll talk to Kane. I'm sure he won't mind."

"Good. Tell you what, let's pop some popcorn and pick out a movie for the VCR."

"Don't you want to work on the remodeling?"

The answer was yes.

He desperately wanted to work on the remodeling, because the sooner he found a way to be farther away from Kate at night, the less temptation he'd have to fight. But he wasn't going to do anything to erase the smile on her face.

"Nah," he lied. "Not tonight. I'm in the mood to play couch potato."

They argued in their old teasing way over which movie to watch. Kate liked classic films, while Dylan preferred science fiction. They finally settled on *When Worlds Collide*, an early sci-fi flick. They'd watched it before, and he had his usual good time poking fun at the special effects, while she critiqued the relationship between the hero and heroine.

It was the way things should have been from the day he'd moved into the carriage house, but then he'd kissed her and everything had gone to hell.

"You do know that movie won an Academy Award for special effects, right?" she asked as the credits rolled up the screen.

"I heard that, then dismissed it as vicious gossip."

Kate rolled her eyes. "I'm sure they were impressive at the time. You're just spoiled by *Star Wars* and all that fancy computer stuff they can do now. But sooner or later even *Star Wars* is going to look outdated."

Dylan lifted an eyebrow at Kate. "Bite your tongue, woman. *Star Wars* is sacred. It will live forever."

She threw an unpopped piece of popcorn at him and

he felt good for the first time in days. Then his gaze drifted to the snug fit of her T-shirt and desire shrank his comfort zone back to zero.

How could he be lusting after Katydid?

It was quite pleasant. If you'd like to do it again, I'd like that, as well.

She'd invited him into her bedroom, something he'd tried to forget. But forgetting he could make love to her again was impossible. It kept him awake at night, distracted him at work, and had sent him to the store to stock up on protection.

Protection?

Dylan snorted to himself. That was locking the barn door after the horse had been stolen, because for the first time in his life he'd failed to use anything when making love to a woman. Could Kate be pregnant?

His mouth went dry at the possibility, but he wasn't sure if it was panic or something more primitive. He wanted her so badly, and it was becoming obvious to him that he'd wanted her for a long time. But she'd always seemed so unattainable, he'd never let himself think about her that way.

"That was fun," Kate said, smiling sleepily as she turned off the TV and VCR with the remote control. "But I'd better clean the kitchen before I end up spending the night here."

"You go to bed, I'll take care of it," Dylan said, shaking his head. He'd gotten into the habit of helping with the dishes every night, but she never took his assistance for granted.

"You don't have to do that."

"You don't have to cook breakfast, lunch and dinner for me, either," he reminded gently. "But you keep insisting."

Kate shrugged. "I'd cook for myself, anyway, and how much trouble is it to add a steak or lamb chop? Besides, you work so hard."

"So do you."

She blinked. "But I don't…you know, have a regular job."

Dylan shook his head. Kate might not have regular punch-the-time-clock sort of work, but she dedicated long hours to her community concerns, and he knew she wasn't just browsing the Web the way she claimed. Anyone with so much concern for others didn't have time to spend that way.

"You work," he said firmly. "Lately you've been gone nearly every evening because of that blessed hospital board."

Once again he felt annoyed, even cheated because of Kate's dedication. Wasn't that a laugh? He'd tried to keep his distance from her, and now he resented it when she wasn't around. No wonder his sisters rolled their eyes and talked with disgust about male irrationality.

"Things should ease up now that the board has voted," Kate murmured. She stretched and untucked her legs from under her. "But I'll take you up on the offer. See you in the morning."

Kate walked into her bedroom and leaned against the door, trying to control her breathing. Dylan had acknowledged that she worked hard. And the way he'd looked at her…

She didn't know what it meant, but it seemed good.

Her skin was so sensitized, she couldn't bear to wear one of her nightshirts, so she crawled into bed naked.

It didn't help the burning need in her abdomen, but it felt good. Sensuous. A reminder of Dylan's lovemaking. Moonlight shone through the windows, splintered by the wavery old glass, and she laid her hand in a shaft of silver light, palm up, trying to capture any magic it might hold.

Moonlight was magical.

It belonged to lovers and fairies and leprechauns. As a child she'd poured her heart out to the moon, so it knew all her secrets.

Faint sounds came from the kitchen, distracting Kate, and she sighed. The movie had been fun, though she didn't know what had prompted Dylan to suggest it. Maybe he just wanted the old times back, before she'd complicated everything by asking him to marry her.

She'd just begun to doze off when her door opened and Dylan approached the bed. Her eyes shot open, and she was suddenly wide awake.

"Kate?" he murmured.

"Y-yes?"

"Did you mean what you said about us? About being interested in…?" His voice trailed, but she knew what he was asking.

Her pulse rate doubled, and she wasn't certain she could talk. Actions seemed as good as words, though, so she lifted the blankets in an inviting gesture.

Apparently it was enough.

Moving with blurring speed, Dylan shed his clothes, but instead of getting under the sheet with her, he grabbed the bedding and flung it to the foot of the bed.

Kate closed her eyes, knowing she was revealed in the silver light. Perhaps not as fully as during the day, but in a way she couldn't hide. Her figure was all right, but nothing spectacular, and he must have been with women who made her look pretty inadequate by comparison.

"Dylan?"

"Don't." He put a finger on her lips and a part of her understood. He didn't want to talk, he only wanted their two bodies, moving together in the night.

Lightly, gently, he touched her.

Every bit of her.

Places she'd never imagined being touched, and it seemed to strip away any inhibitions. After a while she longed for a bolder caress, the tension building unbearably. As if he'd read her mind, Dylan's fingers became more demanding. Without a word he taught her what he enjoyed the most and let her explore her own pleasure.

But he always led the way, never out of control until that last moment when the endless pulses of his release stripped everything else away.

Tears streaked Kate's cheek and she was still trembling, trying to gather herself, when Dylan swung his legs onto the floor and gathered his clothes.

A moment later he closed the door behind him.

Kate doodled on the pad of paper in front of her, trying to look interested in yet another hospital board meeting.

Unfortunately she had other things on her mind.

It had been over five weeks since the night Dylan had slipped into her room to make love…and every night since.

She'd thought marriage to Dylan was the answer to her prayers, but now things seemed more impossible than ever. She was trying to follow his lead when it came to making love, but he seemed to want one thing at night, another during the day.

Nobody who saw them chatting over breakfast or washing dishes after dinner would guess that a few hours later they'd be naked in bed, moving together, over and over, until they were limp and sated and barely able to stir a muscle.

Except Dylan *did* stir.

He'd leave without saying anything.

Her life was now divided between sensual, wordless nights of passion, and friendly, distant days.

"Be sure to thank both your husband and brother-in-law for us, Mrs. O'Rourke," urged the hospital director, Leon Freeman.

"I will." Kate forced a smile to her stiff lips.

"Well, your marriage has certainly proved advantageous to the hospital," said Brian Wayland. "With first your husband and then your brother-in-law making such generous donations."

A wry smile tugged at Kate's mouth. Apparently her own value was now relegated to making an advantageous marriage.

As the meeting broke up and they walked out to their cars, Leon Freeman caught up with her. "Is everything all right, Katrina?" he asked. "You haven't seemed yourself lately."

"Oh…" Kate shook her head. "I'm fine. Adjusting to marriage, I guess."

Leon's kind, dark eyes regarded her with gentle understanding. "Change is never easy. Even good change."

She wished she could talk to him, but she couldn't.

There wasn't anyone she could talk to. Not Dylan, not his family. Not anyone. It was odd, now that she was married, she felt more alone than at any time in her life.

"Don't worry, Leon. I've loved Dylan for so long, it's a dream come true being together."

"Yes. I've heard such excellent things about Mr. O'Rourke. They say he's the most honest builder in the state. Are you certain he won't consider bidding on the hospital? Having a company with his reputation would be a blessing."

"Very certain," Kate said. "Dylan feels it wouldn't look right considering my position on the board and the donation of his company's time for the building demolition."

"I suppose, but it's still a shame. Give him my best."

Kate nodded and got into the new car Dylan had talked her into accepting a few weeks before. It was a shiny silver Volkswagen Passat, but she missed her old Beetle. She'd earned the money for the Beetle herself, and it was a symbol of her independence from her family's wealth.

Back at the carriage house she felt so exhausted she decided to lie down for a while. Her energy level was nonexistent these days, no doubt the result of stress. Or it might be from lack of sleep, she mused as she curled up on the bed.

Dylan's stamina was astonishing.

When Dylan came in that evening he was surprised to find the house virtually silent.

"Kate?" he called.

More silence greeted him, and he put a reluctant hand on her bedroom door. Lately Kate had become withdrawn and quiet, and her eyes haunted him at the oddest moments. He wondered if she regretted the impulsive decision that had tied them together for a year, yet her response to their lovemaking became more passionate every night.

Just thinking about *how* passionate gave Dylan trouble breathing.

The bedroom was lit only by tree-dappled light from the window, and he saw Kate lying on the bed, her left hand stretched out, palm up. She slept that way. Sometimes he peeked in, long after leaving her, and she would have turned over on her side and stretched out an arm.

"Katydid," he whispered, his throat aching with suppressed emotion. He hated seeing her so solemn and pale. She'd always been the sparkle in his life, a beautiful, joyous creature who made him laugh, even when he was a too-serious boy, conscious of his hand-me-down clothing.

Had she realized he had never been anything special? Did she regret them becoming intimate? The thought was a knife cutting into his heart.

Dylan pulled a blanket over Kate, careful not to disturb her. He would have to spend more nights at the office; it was the only way he could keep his hands off her. It would be best for both of them.

Except he didn't want to stay away—not now, not ever. But how could he tell Kate? They had an agreement.

One year.

Chapter Eleven

"**Y**ou don't look like you're getting any sleep," teased Shannon at Sunday dinner. "You must be doing a lot of honeymooning."

Kate smiled obediently.

She *wasn't* getting any sleep.

Dylan hadn't been home for several nights in a row, though he'd finally returned Friday evening. Once again he didn't offer an explanation, and this time she didn't ask because she was angry.

Mostly angry.

In all honesty she didn't have any right to ask. Becoming intimate hadn't given her any claim to Dylan's life.

"Actually, Kate's been working herself sick on the hospital board," Dylan said. He put his arm around her waist and pulled her closer on the couch. "Because of her there's going to be a new children's orthopedic clinic."

He sounded so proud that Kate searched his face, trying to discover if he was putting on an act for the benefit of his family or if he really thought she had done a good job.

"I'm just a small part of making it happen," she murmured.

"Don't believe her," Dylan declared. "Kate is amazing."

The O'Rourkes smiled happily, though Pegeen's gaze seemed to linger longer than necessary on her son and newest daughter-in-law. She was a wise woman and Kate wondered if she'd guessed the truth. Would she believe Kate had never meant to hurt anyone, least of all Dylan?

"I'm afraid Dylan is giving me too much credit. He doesn't really see—"

"Yes, I do." He looked down and cupped her jaw in his palm. His eyes were darkly intent, as if determined to make her understand. "I do see."

It was everything Kate could do not to cry. It didn't seem to be part of his adoring husband act, and she wanted more than anything to believe that he no longer thought of her as a spoiled heiress who dabbled in philanthropy out of boredom. She wanted to be the kind of wife he deserved.

She rested her cheek on his shoulder and listened to the O'Rourkes chatter with one another. It was like a family reunion every week, with food and laughter and good talk. Sooner or later someone always set up a board game and they'd amicably compete. Normally she loved to join in, but her tiredness was genuine. She'd made an appointment with the doctor on Tuesday to get a checkup, but already suspected the cause.

"Do you want to go home?" Dylan murmured, still holding her close.

"No, I'm fine. You were going to build new shelves for your mother's pantry," Kate said, straightening. "Why don't you go ahead, unless you wanted to play a game. I see Maddie just pulled out Monopoly."

Dylan's nose wrinkled. "The last time we played Monopoly I was here until midnight. I'd much rather build those shelves than pass go two million times."

He went outside to get the wood from the back of his truck, and Kate pushed the curtains to one side to watch him put heavy loads on one shoulder, then carry them easily around the back of the house. Lord, he was strong, and not the least bit afraid of hard work.

Her heart aching, Kate got up and skirted the game players who'd settled down for some serious competition.

It was an unusually warm afternoon for the Seattle area, and Dylan had discarded his shirt as he measured and cut boards to their proper length. Muscles moved smoothly beneath his tanned skin and a different kind of warmth invaded Kate's body. As if sensing her watching, he looked up.

"Did you change your mind? Mom won't mind if I do this another time."

"Uh, no. I just wanted some fresh air." She also wanted *him*, but it was hardly the time or place to say so. They had a strange, dichotomous life—friends during the day, and silent, passionate lovers in the dark.

The shelves went together so quickly it amazed Kate, though it shouldn't have. Dylan was transforming the new rooms in the carriage house with breathtaking speed, though she didn't know why he'd decided to do the work himself, rather than bring in a crew who would have finished the remodel in a few days.

Before long the new shelves were coated with glistening white primer and he was telling his mother that he'd return in a couple of days to apply a second coat of paint.

"I can do that, dear," Pegeen protested. "Or it can wait until next weekend."

"Nope. What's the good of having a contractor in the family if you don't let him handle this sort of stuff?" Dylan said, cleaning his hands with turpentine.

"But I don't want to take advantage." Pegeen's eyes were soft with love. "And you've a wife, now, darlin'."

"I know." Dylan looked at Kate perched on a stool and his heart wrenched.

A year.

Kate was his wife for a year.

Once again she hadn't said anything about his four-night absence or objected when he'd been unable to resist slipping into her bedroom after midnight on Saturday. It didn't add up. Kate wasn't the type to take sex lightly. But wanting to believe it meant something and *knowing* it did were two different things.

It made him feel out of control, as if he were trapped in a riptide, with him grabbing at the ground and trying to keep from getting sucked away. Then Kate slipped her hand into his as they said goodbye, and the world was suddenly anchored.

Hell, he was in big trouble. Falling in love wasn't part of their agreement. Of course, he'd fallen in love with her a long time ago, but had just been too stubborn and afraid of losing her to accept it.

When he lifted Kate into the truck, he frowned. "You've lost weight."

"I needed to lose a few pounds."

Dylan stared. "No, you didn't. What's going on?"

She shrugged. "I've been busy, that's all."

"Skipping meals isn't going to help you get more done," he said, exasperated. "I mean it, Kate. You've got to take better care of yourself."

"I don't need a keeper."

"That's not what I said. Listen, honey, I know how much you care about everyone, especially about folks who can't help themselves, but you can't fix all their problems overnight."

Honey?

Kate automatically looked around the yard to see if any of the O'Rourkes had appeared, but they were alone. There wasn't any need to put on an act or utter meaningless endearments.

Honey.

Hope filled her, just because of a little word. But it wasn't just that. It was the way he seemed to understand how important her community work was to her. And that she worked hard.

"The hospital is getting the clinic, and there's money for the day care center…you've done lots of great stuff," Dylan argued. "Making yourself sick isn't going to help anyone else."

"I'm not getting sick."

I just think I'm pregnant.

It was the most likely explanation for her seesawing emotions and tiredness. Dylan had been careful about protection after their first night together, but once was all it took.

She didn't know how she was going to tell him if she

turned out to be right. Getting pregnant wasn't part of their agreement. Of course, sex hadn't been part of the agreement, either, but he'd probably still blame her.

Men were funny that way.

When it came to making babies a lot of them seemed to think a woman did it all by herself.

"I have a checkup with the doctor this week," she told Dylan. "So you don't have to worry about me."

"But I do worry." His hands stroked her thighs in slow circles. It was the first time since they'd first made love that he'd really touched her outside of bed, and her toes curled. "But it isn't because I don't think you can take care of yourself, though you do tend to think of others first."

"Not bad for a spoiled brat, right?"

"You're not spoiled." Dylan's dark gaze lifted, and he seemed to be asking or saying something. "I'm sorry I ever thought that, because it was never true."

Kate swallowed and blinked. Drat her hormones, this was no time to cry. "I've never been denied anything. Most people would consider that spoiled."

"Wrong, you were denied *everything* you wanted," he corrected gently. "You wanted your parents and grandmother to love you unconditionally. You wanted to be held and comforted and remembered in the good times and the bad. You wanted to give the same love back, and they wouldn't take it. But it wasn't because of you, sweetheart, it was because they couldn't see past the emptiness in their lives."

Oh, dear.

He did understand. She'd never had someone see her so well, and it was both wonderful and scary at the same time.

"Dylan…" Her voice caught and two tears escaped.

"Don't cry, Katydid." Dylan wiped them away and left kisses in their place. "I know things are mixed up right now, and I'm a big part of making it that way. But it's going to be all right. We'll sort it out."

If she could only believe that, but he'd be so angry when he found out she'd tricked him.

Kate thought about it through the week, particularly at the doctor's office when the physician prescribed prenatal vitamins and told her to drink more milk and take a nap every afternoon.

By Friday she was no closer to an answer, and she finally walked over to the Douglas Hill House, partly to make notes on the restoration needed, but mostly to confront her past.

The enormous foyer echoed as Kate opened the door, and she shivered. Visits had always been times of disapproval or of stern lectures on how a Douglas should properly behave.

"Sorry, Grandmamma," Kate said. "But I'm too much like Grandfather Rycroft—I don't want to be buried before I start living."

No answer came, and she shook her head. Her imagination had been another source of Jane Douglas's displeasure, but her imagination, and Dylan, had been the saving graces of her childhood.

The afternoon wore on as Kate completed page after page of notes. Her grandmother had become notoriously tight with money in the last two decades of her life. A great deal of work would be needed if Kate succeeded in establishing the Douglas Hill House Historical Foundation.

In one of the neglected second floor bedrooms on the north of the house Kate shut the door to examine a crack in the wall, but when she tried to open it the ancient knob just turned without doing anything. She shook the knob and tried it again without success.

"Tarnation."

She kicked the heavy mahogany door, then tried everything she could think of to get the knob to catch whatever it was supposed to catch on. She even tried removing the whole assembly, but her fingernails couldn't budge the screws.

"I can't believe this," Kate muttered, prowling around the room. The bathroom worked, though the fixtures were right out of the nineteen twenties. "Why didn't I bring my cell phone?"

Dylan would be home soon, so she forced a window open and looked out. Great. Just great. There was no way to climb down safely. Almost as bad, the carriage house was tucked behind a stand of trees on the other side of the mansion. Dylan wouldn't hear her, no matter how hard she yelled.

Nevertheless, Kate called and shouted off and on until her throat was raw, then she threw herself down on the dusty bed and glared at the massive four-poster.

Fine. Dylan could wonder where *she* was for once.

Of course, he might realize something was wrong when she didn't call. She wasn't in any danger, but it would be nice if he'd worry enough to come looking.

Dylan got back to the carriage house later than normal, but it was for a good reason and he didn't think Kate would mind.

"That's fine," he called, directing his companions to park in front of the house.

"Your wife is gonna love this," said the man who'd driven Kate's fully restored Beetle back from the shop. He ran a hand over the shiny fire-engine red hood. "It was mostly the body that needed work, the motor runs great."

Dylan grimaced. He would have to eat crow with Kate. The mechanics had raved about the beautifully maintained condition of the working parts of her car. How many times had he assumed she couldn't take care of herself, when all along she was doing it quietly and well?

"Can I wait to see Mrs. O'Rourke's reaction?"

"No, you can't," said the third man who'd followed them. "They become like his babies," he said to Dylan, shaking his head. "Come on, Fred, it's time to cut the cord."

Dylan escorted them down to the gate, then hurried back to the house, hoping Kate hadn't gotten curious about the commotion in the driveway.

The Beetle sat in the evening sunlight, looking like it had just rolled off the assembly line. He'd tell Kate it was her real birthday present and that she could forget he'd ever bought that stupid pair of earrings.

Pleased, Dylan ran up the stairs. Kate was probably in the kitchen, fixing another one of her inevitable salads, and seasoning a steak for him to eat. He was getting pretty damn spoiled by all that.

Tonight he'd try to get her to eat some of the steak herself. He didn't care that the doctor claimed she was in good health. Her weight loss bothered him. It bothered him even more that she might have lost weight because of something he'd done.

"Kate? I have a surprise for you."

The house was silent. Was she taking another nap? Remembering the day he'd come home to find her asleep, he peeked into the bedroom, then frowned. It was empty.

Trying not to worry, Dylan checked the phone machine, then called his office voice mail.

Nothing.

The car he'd bought for her was in the garage, but that didn't mean anything. She might have taken a cab or been picked up by a friend or a fellow board member, and if she was in the middle of a sensitive negotiation she might not feel free to break off for a phone call. He'd order some Chinese food and have it waiting when she got here. No way would he let her cook at the end of such a long day.

Four hours later Dylan was climbing the walls.

He would have liked to believe Kate was just getting back at him for his own overnight absences, but that wasn't her style. Before they were married he might have believed she was immature enough to want revenge, but not now. He'd gotten to know her better. Or had he?

As the minutes ticked by, Dylan tried to figure out what he should do, and realized he didn't know Kate at all. They'd been as intimate in the bedroom as two people could be, but he didn't know who her friends were, or where her interests lay, or anything else. He didn't even know who to start calling. Why had he wasted so much time, not talking to Kate and getting to really know her?

"Damn."

Dylan rooted around in Kate's desk. There were plans to the Douglas Hill House spread out everywhere, so he pushed them out of the way and kept searching until he found an address book. It was late, but he didn't care. It was more important to find his wife.

Picking up the phone, he flipped to A and started dialing.

"Kate?"

Kate woke up reluctantly, vaguely aware of her name being called. She felt grubby and hungry, yet calmer than she'd felt in weeks. With nothing to do all night but think, she'd come to a difficult decision—no more deception, no more hiding the way she felt about Dylan. It might mean the end of their friendship, but he deserved the truth.

Maybe she should have told him from the beginning. Dylan kept everything bottled up inside, and if he saw her putting her heart and pride on the line, it could make a difference. If he loved her, he loved her.

"Katydid, are you here?"

"Dylan?"

Dust motes stirred in the air as she scrambled from the bed and ran to the door.

"Dylan, I'm in here. The latch is broken."

A moment later the knob spun as he attempted to open it, with no more success than she'd found. Some creative cursing sounded, though it was muffled by the heavy wood door, and a weary smile crossed her face.

"You'll have to get some tools," she said. "I didn't have anything to use except my fingernails."

"Just get back, I'm going to kick it in."

Kate was too tired to argue. "Okay, I'm back," she called, waiting near the bed.

Dylan's kick was so powerful the door hit the wall and bounced back in his face.

"Are you all right?" he demanded, striding inside and grabbing her shoulders. "I've been going crazy trying to find you. I finally realized the floor plans of the mansion in your room might mean that you'd come over here. I'm sorry it took me so long to figure it out."

"I'm fine."

His concern warmed her heart, but it couldn't change her decision. She had to tell him before she lost her nerve or before she could be tempted to let things go any further.

"We have to talk," she blurted out.

His forehead crinkled in a frown. "Yes, I know. But not now. I'm going to get you back to the house so you can get something to eat and some decent rest."

"No, Dylan, we have to talk now. It can't wait."

"Honey, this is crazy. You're obviously exhausted."

A choked sob came out of her throat. "Please, this isn't easy for me."

Something in Kate's expression caught Dylan's attention and he went cold. "Yes?" he asked cautiously.

"The thing is, I wasn't being fair, asking you to marry me. I think we should file for a divorce right away so you can get back to your life."

"You...*what*?" Dylan couldn't believe his ears. Of all the things he'd expected to hear once he found her, being asked for a divorce wasn't one of them.

"You heard me," Kate whispered.

"Uh, if this is about us making love, I feel bad

enough about abusing your trust. It won't happen again." It was a promise Dylan hoped he could keep, because he'd never had so much trouble keeping his hands to himself.

"It's not about that."

"Then what *is* it about?" His emotions, already charged by a sleepless night and frantic worry, exploded in anger. "If you want a divorce, you're going to have to file for it yourself, Katydid. I may not be the sort of husband you want, but if we separate before the year is up, you're going to lose the house."

"The house doesn't matter," she said miserably. "I don't care about it. I never did."

Dylan stared. "You…don't?"

"No. I don't need an inheritance or a husband to support me. I make a good living writing children's books. As for making love, I'm very capable of saying no, so you aren't any more responsible for what happened than I am."

He shook his head. "I don't get it."

Kate wrapped her arms around her stomach. She felt cold, but it was mostly fear, not the chill of the old house and early morning air.

"There's nothing to get. It's very simple. I tricked you into marrying me. You see, I've been in love with you for so very long, but you refused to see that I'd grown up. So when Grandmamma died and put that ridiculous codicil in her will, I used it as an excuse."

Dylan listened, shock and wonder struggling in his chest.

Kate loved him?

Once upon a time he might have doubted her feelings, but he'd learned too much about her passionate, loving nature. She wouldn't say that she loved him if she didn't mean it with all her heart.

"I love you, too," he said quietly.

"You're just saying that because you're so used to taking care of me. Didn't you hear me? I tricked you."

He sighed, wishing he'd been smarter and faster figuring things out. His mother was right. He *had* forgotten to listen to his heart, but he was listening now. And one of the things he heard, like a warm, healing tide, was his father's wisdom. He didn't know if Keenan had really spoken to him weeks ago in the garden, but somehow he thought it was true.

"The codicil is real. You had to get married or lose the house."

"I told you I don't care about the house," she exclaimed. "The historical society is going to run it as a nonprofit foundation."

Dylan grinned.

That was more like Kate. He should have known she wouldn't want Douglas Hill House for herself. It was too pretentious and stuffy. Anybody who'd drive that former rust bucket of a car wouldn't give two figs for a brooding old mansion.

As for her deception, he *was* a little annoyed about it, but things had turned out well, so it seemed ungrateful to complain. He could forgive her, if that's what she wanted.

"Honey, it's all right, it doesn't matter how it happened."

"It doesn't?"

"No. I knew something was up, but I went along, anyway. I do, however, have to point out that the house isn't yours for a year. And won't *ever* be yours if we get divorced. Which would be a shame—Seattle could use another museum showpiece like the Pittock Mansion down in Portland. It'll take some work, but my company will help with the restoration."

Kate slapped her forehead. "I wish you'd listen to me."

"I am, honey, I'm finally listening. People have said things about us for years that didn't make sense to me. I guess they recognized the truth I was too stubborn to see, or maybe I just didn't have enough courage to risk losing what we did have for something that might not come true."

Kate trembled. Dylan was probably just saying what he knew she wanted to hear, but she knew how to scare him.

"I'm pregnant, Dylan. You didn't use anything that first night, and I was in my fertile period. I knew it, but I thought you'd used something, and then things got…out of control."

Instead of the panicked, trapped expression she expected, a brilliant smile filled his face. The last time she'd seen him that happy was before his father died.

"You're having our baby?" He touched her tummy with a look of reverence.

"Yes, a baby. Crying in the middle of the night, teething, dirty diapers…the whole thing."

"It's wonderful. I hope it's a girl just like her mother."

She leaned against one of the high bedposts and moaned, wanting to believe him.

"I love you so much it scares me," Dylan murmured, his large hand caressing her abdomen. "I know it's not going to be easy. I have to start talking and listening, especially to you, but you're willing to help, aren't you?"

"Of course, but—"

He put a finger over her mouth. "Listen, Kate. Deep down I've always loved you, but I couldn't accept that a woman like you would ever look at such an ordinary guy. That's why I wanted you to stay a kid…because then you wouldn't really see me."

"I've always seen you," Kate whispered, her throat aching with regret for the lost years. But at least Dylan had acknowledged his feelings and the lingering insecurities of his boyhood, and it gave her hope for the future. "I've seen you better than anyone. You're wonderful. All I've ever wanted is to be with you."

Dylan saw the love and faith in Kate's eyes and pulled her close. "I love you," he whispered. "Don't ever leave me."

"I won't." But all at once she drew back and raised her eyebrows. "Now tell me where you spent all those nights."

He threw back his head and laughed. She'd finally asked. "On my office couch. I thought it would cool things down between us."

Kate tugged on his belt buckle. "You thought wrong. I have years of sleeping alone to make up for, and I don't plan on wasting any time."

"You don't?"

"No."

He eyed the bed. "That's interesting. I've always wanted to make love in a dark, forbidding mansion, in a four-poster bed, after rescuing a sexy woman who miraculously happens to be my wife."

"It was very lonely in that bed last night."

Dylan smiled and gathered her close, finally understanding that was all he'd ever needed to do; his beautiful butterfly would always make sure she was within reach.

"It won't ever be lonely again," he promised against her lips. "You can count on it."

Epilogue

Kate held her baby daughter and smiled proudly as Dylan stood at the podium. The mayor and governor had already given their speeches, then she'd spoken briefly. Now it was his turn.

"Ladies and gentleman, it has been a great privilege to work with my wife in restoring this house to its original condition."

"Hi, Poppa," exclaimed eighteen-month-old Keenan, bouncing up and down in the chair next to Kate. The assembled guests and dignitaries and assorted O'Rourkes laughed.

Dylan grinned. "Hi, son."

Pegeen shushed her grandson and lifted him onto her lap. She was a marvelous grandmother, loving and indulgent, particularly with her hugs and kisses. Her grandkids would never have to wonder if she loved them, and Kate's eyes misted, knowing she'd never have to wonder about that again, either.

"Anybody who knows my lovely wife knows her dedication to the betterment of people's lives, and her passion to preserve the history of our town…" Dylan continued, only to be interrupted by a burst of applause.

Heat flooded Kate's cheeks and she ducked her face over Caitlin's receiving blanket. Honestly, Dylan had promised he wouldn't embarrass her.

"…and today a dream of hers has come true—to offer her family's historic home as a museum and cultural center to the emerald city of Seattle."

More applause broke out, and Kate's gaze locked with Dylan's as he waited. The past three years had been filled with love and laughter and hard work…and the arrival of two very special little people. First Keenan, named for the grandfather he would know only in spirit, and then Caitlin, the daughter who'd already enslaved her poppa with her bright smiles.

Dylan loved being a daddy.

He was already hinting around that in another year or two they could expand their family.

And why not?

The carriage house had plenty of room. Dylan had transformed the entire second floor into a lovely, spacious home. He'd planned everything, including a master bedroom and bath, complete with a whirlpool tub, big enough for two. A tall, wrought iron fence would keep visitors to the mansion away from the house without being too obvious.

"So without further ado, the Douglas Hill House is declared officially open for visitors," Dylan announced.

More cheers and clapping followed, and Kate was immediately surrounded by well-wishers. She looked at her husband through the sea of people and blew him a kiss.

"It's a fine thing you've done here," said Richard Carter, finding her in a more quiet moment.

"I doubt it's what Grandmamma expected me to do with the house."

He sighed. "Your grandmother had many ideas, Katrina, and many expectations. It is questionable that any of them made her happy."

"Darling." Dylan put his arms around both her and Caitlin and kissed her cheek. "Hey, Richard. Glad you could make it."

"I wouldn't have missed the grand opening, Dylan. I toured Hill House a few days ago with the historical society. It's remarkable what you've done in there."

"Yeah, it came out all right."

Dylan kept an arm around Kate as he looked back at the mansion. It no longer brooded, alone and neglected. The formal gardens were carefully restored, with sweeping green lawns and a profusion of fall plantings. Sparkling windows and the restored stone exterior had only been the beginning; they'd stripped and stained and painted, doing much of the work themselves, revealing the enduring spirit of a grand old lady.

He'd grown fond of the mansion, largely because it had helped bring Kate to him. They'd also managed to make love in nearly every room, forever imprinting it with sexy laughter and happy memories. Kate believed houses reflected the lives of their owners. Dylan didn't know if that was true, but in case she was right, they'd done their best to give the Douglas Hill House a good new beginning.

"Poppa."

Dylan laughed as Keenan barreled into his legs. "Hey, buddy." He lifted his son high in the air and settled him on his shoulders.

Keenan chortled and patted his daddy's head.

God, it was great to be alive.

They were eating refreshments in the garden when Kate looked up and stiffened. "It's my father."

Terrific.

Kate still didn't have much of a relationship with Isabelle and Chad Douglas, though Chad had made some effort. He truly seemed to regret missing their wedding and had stopped to visit a few times.

"Hello, Katrina."

"Father. I'm glad you could come. I hope…I hope this is all right with you. We never really talked about it."

Chad looked around the gardens, then back at his childhood home. A strange, almost contorted expression went across his face. "Katrina, do you know why my mother left you the Hill House, instead of me?"

"Not really." Kate moved closer to Dylan and he clasped her hand. It was something she'd wondered about, and she worried her father would object to his family home going on public display.

"It's because I hated it so much. Ever since I was a child."

Kate's eyes widened. "You did?"

"Yes. But somehow it feels different now. By the way, I saw the dedication to Rycroft in the foyer." A smile broke out on Chad's mouth. "I'm glad you made it his again. I just wish he'd hung around long enough to take me with him—I think I would have enjoyed Alaska."

Dylan suddenly found himself liking his father-in-law. "It's never too late, sir."

"No." Chad looked at Kate, then at the baby in her arms, and his grandson playing hide-and-seek beneath a bench. "While it does sound like fun, I'd rather get to know my own family. It turns out I've got a really special daughter."

Kate gulped back tears.

Chad gave her an awkward hug, then kissed her forehead. "Let's go out to lunch soon."

She nodded agreement.

It was a start. That was all anyone could ask for.

Much later, with everything quiet and the children in bed, Kate put her head on Dylan's shoulder and gazed into the fire crackling on the hearth.

"You did a nice job restoring the old cars," she murmured.

He laughed. "They didn't need restoring, just a good coat of wax. But they look good in the garage your great-grandfather built."

"Mmm, yes."

The carriage house had only been used to house the family's old cars, once newer ones had been acquired. In keeping with the historic theme of Hill House, her grandmother's limousine had been relegated to a storage shed, and the Rolls Royce Silver Ghost and Daimler now gleamed in its place. A sophisticated security system guarded the priceless vehicles, much to the relief of the foundation charged with protecting them.

Kate kissed her husband's jaw. "By my calculations, we have just over two hours before Caitlin will demand her next feeding. Do you have any ideas on how we could use that time?"

"I might." His fingers slipped under her blouse and caressed her breasts.

Shimmering warmth spun through her veins. She'd never get tired of it, the loving and holding and passion.

"I love a man who knows how to use his hands," she purred.

Dylan grinned and tossed her blouse and nursing bra over his shoulders. "And the foundation loves having a free handyman, conveniently living on the property."

Kate looked at him seriously. "You don't have to keep doing so much. We've got a resident caretaker and a security staff, and the endowment is more than enough to cover costs. Besides, they know you have O'Rourke Construction to run."

"Hey, if I didn't like it, I'd say so. You're the one who has trouble saying no."

She blushed and put her face on his chest. There were times Kate still reminded Dylan of the little girl she'd once been, and she probably always would, but her body definitely belonged to a woman.

"I love you," he whispered, lifting her chin and looking into her sea green eyes. "I couldn't live without you."

"You never have to."

Their lips met in a sweet kiss, filled with forerunners of desire and a future of hope and love.

Life just didn't get any better.

* * * * *